# IN COLD BLOOD

Clint had tucked the two Colt automatic pistols into his waistband. Liberating one with his left hand, he brought it up to shoulder height after the fashion of a target shooter. Taking aim at where the Ranger was starting to sit up, he squeezed the trigger twice.

Watching, Torreson saw two holes appear in the left breast of Soehnen's calfskin vest as he was slammed backward once more.

"You killed him!" The New Yorker grunted, impressed by the speed by which the deed had been carried out.

"Seemed like a good thing to do," the small Texan replied. "We couldn't've just rode off and left him here to spread that we've gotten away. But I'd have killed him anyways. Nobody knocks down Rapido Clint and lives."

## QUANTITY SALES

# Rapido Clint

## J. T. EDSON

A DELL BOOK

Published by
Dell Publishing
a division of
Bantam Doubleday Dell Publishing Group, Inc.
666 Fifth Avenue
New York, New York 10103

ISBN: 0-440-20868-8

Reprinted by arrangement with the author.

Printed in the United States of America

Published simultaneously in Canada

May 1991

10 9 8 7 6 5 4 3 2 1

OPM

*For Ann's daughters, "Jumping" Julie and "Aerialistic"
Angela, who assure me they are just as 'orrible as Nicola
Gibbon, or even 'orribler and hate me ever more than she does.*

# Rapido Clint

# 1

# TAKE HER APART, DAISY

"Hey, you carrot-topped bitch, those are *my* stockings you're wearing!"

"What did you say, you mother-something gutter slut?"*

"You heard me, you lard-gutted old hay bag.* Those are *my* stockings and I damned well want them back!"

Hearing the heated statement, challenge, and demand, spoken alternatively in a well-educated New England and a much coarser, strident midwestern accent, all the other occupants of the elegantly furnished and red-velvet-draped "reception room" of Minnie Lassiter's Premier Chicken Ranch stopped what they were doing and gazed around with interest. Such comments were not in accord with the standards of behavior demanded by the madam of as fine a brothel as could be found anywhere in Texas. However, the quarrel lent excitement to what was a dull period. As the time was just after one o'clock on a Thursday

* "Hay bag" and "gutter slut" are colloquial names for a low-class prostitute. *J.T.E.*

afternoon, there were no more than half a dozen "clients"—as
Minnie insisted the customers were called—present. So far none
of them had shown any inclination to do anything other than
drink either the beer or hard liquor that was being sold openly
and in defiance of the Volstead Act,* or to partake of the excellent free buffet lunch set out on a table at the left side of the
polished mahogany bar.

Knowing who was disputing the claim to the ownership of
the stockings, the girls who were present did not doubt it was
justified. However, the accusor, who had arrived late the previous evening and retired almost immediately to the room she had
been allocated by the madam, was still an unknown quantity to
them. She had struck the few who had met her at breakfast as
being friendly but uncommunicative about herself. So, having
nothing upon which to base their judgment where she was concerned, past experience made them consider that she was behaving in a most ill-advised fashion under the circumstances.

Red-haired, buxom, yet with little or no flabby fat, good-
looking in a sullen way, thirty-year-old Daisy Extall had established sufficient physical domination over her fellow workers to
enable her to appropriate any items of their property to which
she took a fancy. Hot-tempered, something of a bully, she invariably responded violently to anybody who objected to her
impositions. So she could be counted upon to resent being addressed in such a disrespectful fashion, particularly when she
was sitting with the three most affluent-looking of the potential
customers.

Daisy had on an open negligee of black silk that exposed her

---

* Volstead Act: A colloquial name for the Eighteenth (Prohibition)
Amendment to the Constitution of the United States of America. This
defined intoxicating liquors as those containing more than one-half of 1
percent alcohol and made illegal the manufacture, transportation, and sale
of such liquors for beverage purposes. Introduced by Representative An-
drew J. Volstead of Minnesota, the act was ratified—over the veto of President Woodrow Wilson—on October 18, 1919, and repealed in 1933. *J.T.E.*

bulky, hard-muscled curves encased in a black glove silk- and lace-trimmed envelope chemise with pockets. From beneath its flaring legs emerged her sturdy calves and thighs. The scarlet straps of her garter belt were coupled to the disputed pair of black silk stockings. On her feet were high-heeled red pumps, the toes decorated by pompoms. There was nothing soft, or gentle, about her demeanor. Rather it suggested, with *very* good cause, an arrogant and truculent nature that one would be wise to avoid provoking.

The new girl, who had introduced herself as Rita Ansell, showed no signs of being perturbed or intimidated by the threatening attitude. Matching Daisy's height of five foot six inches, she was some six years younger and possibly ten pounds lighter, although this did not mean that she had a slender build. Contrary to the current trend of fashion that favored a trim and "boyish" type of figure, her bosom was well developed and even firmer than that of the redhead. What was more, as she wore nothing except a pink glove silk brassiere and panties, with white appliqué embroidery,* which left her midriff bare, she exhibited beyond any doubt that her waist trimmed down without the need for artificial aids. She was pretty, without being excessively beautiful, but her face showed grim determination and her brown hair was cut in a short, tousled, curly, "windblown" bob.

"You do, do you, you mother-something ass-peddler?" Daisy yelled. "Well, this is all you'll g—!"

While speaking, the redhead was kicking off her pumps. Having done so, she thrust her chair away as she rose swiftly. Once on her feet, she followed up her favorite profanity by swinging her right fist in a power-packed roundhouse punch at the approaching brunette.

---

* "Appliqué embroidery": Dressmaker's term, from the French, meaning, "applied to." A style of embellishment used on fabrics, lace, net, or leather, and so on, in which cutout motifs are sewn by hand. *J.T.E.*

Her comment was not finished. Nor did the blow land.

Swiveling aside and rapidly bringing up her hands, Rita caught hold of Daisy's right wrist. Such was the strength with which the redhead was being gripped that, especially as she was taken unawares, she could not prevent the trapped arm from being twisted behind her back in a painful fashion. Then she was given a powerful shove which confirmed her suspicion that the brunette was far from being a puny, flabby weakling. In fact, she concluded that she could be dealing with somebody almost able to match her own strength. Sent across the room in a reeling rush, Daisy was brought to a halt and saved from falling only by her arrival at the counter. Spitting out more vile language, she turned to find Rita was coming toward her in a way that invited the kind of reprisal that had served her well in the past.

Bending at the waist and blessing her foresight that had made her remove the pumps, which would have been more of a liability than an asset under the circumstances, Daisy thrust herself away from the bar. Although Rita realized what was coming and tried to counter it by turning her advance into a retreat, she was only partially successful. The boyishly short shingle-cut red hair offered little cushioning effect as Daisy's head rammed into her bosom, but the impact would have been far worse if she had not commenced the attempted evasion. As it was, gasping with pain, she went back a few steps to trip and sit down hard on the floor. Darting after her, Daisy launched a kick at her head.

Once again the brunette showed how quickly and capably she could respond to danger by grabbing the approaching ankle in both hands before its foot could reach her. Giving a twisting heave on the captured limb, she caused the redhead to stumble away. Managing to remain erect, by the time she had regained sufficient control over her movements to halt the turn, the red-head found Rita was almost standing. For a moment they glared at each other. Then they began to move forward on a converging course.

"Go get her, new gal!" whooped one of the three young men

clad in the attire of cowhands who had been drinking beer by the free lunch counter when the trouble started. They watched the brunette charging at the redhead.

"Take her apart, Daisy!" suggested the largest and heaviest of the trio with whom the woman in question had been keeping company. Although he wore a good three-piece suit and a white shirt, like his companions, he had removed his collar and necktie. The reddening of his surly features and his somewhat slurred tone suggested he had taken a couple more drinks than was wise. "Strip her buff naked and stomp her good!"

While the rest of the clients also raised their voices in vigorous encouragement, the watching girls remained silent. The absence of comment on their part was caused by caution rather than disinterest. So far the newcomer had shown to good advantage, but they knew the fight was not yet over. Should Daisy emerge victorious, as had happened on every other occasion except one since her arrival at the Premier Chicken Ranch, she would take reprisals against anybody she had heard giving vocal support to her defeated opponent. Lacking any evidence upon which to base a judgment where Rita was concerned, they were aware that she might react in the same fashion if she was able to overcome the redhead. So, although they were watching with an even greater attention than any of the customers, they considered it was politic not to allow their sentiments to become known to either combatant.

Upon arriving within reaching distance, Rita and Daisy shot out their hands. Eager fingers dug as deeply as possible into fashionably short hair, tugging and jerking savagely. Spinning across the room in such a fashion, they kicked indiscriminately at one another's legs. Each retained her grasp on the other's locks, to the accompaniment of squeals and yells of anger, for several seconds. However, the onlookers' hopes for a long and decisive fight did not materialize.

In fact, the combatants were not even granted an opportunity to either change to more effective tactics or inflict any damage.

Attracted by the commotion, the madam of the establishment hurried through the door of her private office. Despite having asked him to stay behind, she was followed by the man with whom she had been discussing business.

Not quite five foot nine in height, Minnie Lassiter was in her late forties and carried her age exceptionally well. Any gray that might have come to her Dutch cut bobbed hair was concealed by having had it dyed silver blond, while carefully applied makeup masked whatever lines and wrinkles assailed her beautiful yet imperious face. As always during working hours, she was exquisitely and tastefully jeweled. The light-blue satin dinner pajamas she was wearing set off her willowy figure to its best advantage, but the bell bottoms of the trousers were so extensive in cut and hung sufficiently low to prevent any sign of her footwear showing.

Taking in the sight, Minnie gave a low cluck of annoyance. Not only did she disapprove of the girls reducing their earning power by fighting, she was aware of the danger inherent in allowing the present fracas to continue. The combatants' adherents might decide to respond with more than just verbal support and a full-scale brawl could ensue to the detriment of the furnishings and fittings. Without as much as a glance at her visitor, although she knew he would be most interested in what was taking place, she darted rather than walked across the reception room. Her movements were similar to the menacing glide of a great cat stalking its prey.

Long experience as a madam had taught Minnie the quickest and safest way to deal with such a situation. On reaching the embattled pair, who were so engrossed in each other that neither was aware of her arrival—although Daisy ought to have been alert to such an eventuality—Minnie's methods proved simple and very effective. After thrusting forward her hands, she grasped them by the scruffs of their necks. Giving neither time to realize the danger, much less attempt to resist, she dragged them a short way apart with no discernible difficulty for all her slender build. Then she jerked them inward just as sharply and forcefully. Their foreheads came together with a click that resembled two king-sized billiard balls kissing. Instantly all their respective aggressive tendencies ended and they both went limp. On being released, they collapsed to sprawl side by side, motionless. Gazing dispassionately down at them, the madam brushed the palms of her hands against one another in a gesture of disdain.

"Aw shit, Minnie!" the burly man in the suit protested indignantly. "Why the something hell didn't you let them have it out to a something finish?"

"Because I don't approve of such unladylike behavior in my house, *Mr.* Molyneux!" the madam replied, her voice haughty and chilling, with the accent of a well-educated Southerner. "Nor, as I have had cause to tell you-all before, do I condone such language and overfamiliarity on the part of *guests* under my roof. So I would suggest, *sir,* that you and your friends finish your drinks and take your departure."

"Are you telling *me* to get out?" the man demanded indignantly.

"I'm telling you-all just *that!*" Minnie confirmed, her manner implying there was no point in further discussion. Paying not the slightest attention to the scowling client, she swung her gaze to the girls. "Take Miss Extall and Miss Ansell to their rooms, please, ladies. Keep them apart. I will speak with them later."

"Well, what do you know about that?" asked the man who had followed the madam from her office, watching some of the girls carrying the unconscious brunette and redhead toward the stairs. "Those two could be—"

Despite wearing a waist-length black *bolero* jacket with silver filigree patterning on it, a frilly bosomed white silk shirt, a Navajo silver and turquoise bolo tie, and brown doeskin trousers— the legs of which flared at the bottom and were inlet by inverted V-shaped slits to display high-heeled, sharp-toed, bulky spur-carrying riding boots—all suggestive of Mexican manufacture,

the speaker's features were undoubtedly Caucasian. Six foot in
height, brown haired, clean shaven, tanned and ruggedly good-
looking, his accent was indicative of having spent his formative
years on the Lower East Side of New York. Many a policeman
of that city would have identified him as Victor Torreson and, if
conscientious, would have attempted to place him under arrest
for the various crimes—including at least one rape and four
cold-blooded murders—he was known to have committed there.

"I *asked* you to keep out of sight!" Minnie snapped, *sotto
voce,* interrupting the comment before it could be completed.

"Why?" the man from New York inquired, favoring the half a
dozen clients—who were already resuming their activities—
with a contemptuous jerk of his left thumb. "None of these
rubes know me and, even if—"

"Possibly not!" Minnie replied, stalking by her visitor. "But
my motto has always been 'Better safe than sorry.' Come back
immediately."

"What's up?" Torreson challenged, following the madam into
the office and watching her close the door behind them with an
annoyed gesture. "I thought you had the local bulls in your
pocket."

"That is something of an exaggeration, unfortunately," Minnie admitted, crossing to sit behind her large and costly-looking
desk. "Being established beyond the city limits, I'm outside the
jurisdiction of the El Paso Police Department. And, while Sheriff Tragg allows me to continue doing business unimpeded, it is
on the clear understanding that I keep an orderly house." Raising her left hand in a prohibitive gesture as her visitor opened
his mouth, she went on. *"Please,* don't say *anything* about an
'orderly disorderly house,' I've heard it so *many* times before.
Our arrangement hardly constitutes having him 'in my pocket,'
as you called it. In fact, knowing him rather well, I doubt
whether he would regard my entertaining a fugitive badly
wanted by the New York Police Department at all favorably.
Nor would the Texas Rangers!"

"Who's going to tell them I'm here?" Torreson demanded, his voice threatening.

"Nobody, I hope," Minnie answered, showing no sign of being disturbed or alarmed by her visitor's hostile demeanor. "For *both* our sakes. Dear Mr. Hogan Turtle would be *most* put out if he had to be told the Premier Chicken Ranch was closed as a result of either the sheriff or the Rangers learning you were here."

"Like I said," Torreson said with a growl. "Who's to squeal?" A frown came to his face and he glanced at the door through which he had just entered, then continued. "Or is one of those tubes a stool pigeon?"

"Not to the best of my knowledge," the madam asserted, then she anticipated the fugitive's next question before it could be uttered. "Nor are any of my people. But that doesn't mean you couldn't have been seen, or that word might have leaked out that you intended to come here. In which case, either the sheriff or the Rangers would come after you."

"There's *that!*" Torreson conceded, slouching toward the chair he had occupied and from the back of which his wide-rimmed, high-crowned white *sombrero* was suspended by its fancy *barbiquejo* chin strap. "But I thought you said those spotters out front and at the back would see any bulls who were coming in plenty of time for me to lam out of here and get back across the river?"

"They've never failed me in the past," Minnie declared as the fugitive threw a look at the office's second door—which gave access to the outside of the house—and appeared to be contemplating a hurried departure. "In fact, the law has never considered it practical, or worthwhile, to try and raid me. But that is no reason for giving them a motive by flouting your presence here unnecessarily."

"All right, already!" Torreson said, but forced himself to sound more amiable than he was feeling. "I'll keep out of sight until I go."

The New Yorker's conciliatory attitude was because he wa
reminded of the madam's connections with the current head o
a family that had been prominent in the criminal activities o
Texas even prior to the winning of independence from Mexica
domination in 1836.*

Galling as the thought might be to Torreson, he was aware o
exactly how important to the future of himself and his associate
was the continued good relations between themselves and Ho
gan Turtle's organization. So he made himself adopt a mor
polite manner than would otherwise have been the case whe
dealing with the madam of a brothel, even one as well know
and liked as Minnie Lassiter. Not only did he remember havin
been informed that she was held in high esteem by Turtle, bu
the incident he had just witnessed in the reception room led hin
to assume she could fulfill the special requirements that ha
caused him to take the chance of crossing the international bor
der.

"Very well, sit down again, please," the madam responded
She was confident that she could supply her visitor's needs, bu
she considered it advisable to let him know what powerful card
she was holding. When he had sat down she went on. "Now
what were you saying out there?"

"Those two twists you stopped fighting—" the New Yorke
commenced.

"Unbecoming though their behavior might have been, Mr
Torreson," Minnie cut in, "I prefer *not* to hear my young ladie
referred to as *twists*!"

* Information regarding two earlier heads of the family, Coleman and hi
son Rameses "Ram" Turtle, can be found in: *Ole Devil and The Caplocks*—
which, along with the other volumes in the Ole Devil Hardin series, cover
aspects of the Texans' struggle to obtain independence from rule by Mexic
—*Set Texas Back on Her Feet* (Berkley Medallion Books 1978 edition re
titled *Viridian's Trail*); *Beguinage* and *Beguinage Is Dead!* Also, by infer
ence, in: Part Four, "Mr. Colt's Revolving Cylinder Pistol, *J.T.'S Hur
dredth* and *The Quest for Bowie's Blade. J.T.E.*

"I'll keep it in mind," the fugitive answered, concluding that is hostess must be very confident of her standing in Hogan urtle's organization to be adopting such a high-handed attitude ith him. Aware of how much depended on retaining her coop- ration, he contrived to keep any suggestion of annoyance or icetiousness from his voice and he went on almost mildly. "The ning is, from what I saw out there, they could be just what the oss wants for his party."

"They *could* be, I suppose," Minnie seconded, giving no indi- ation that she had already reached a similar conclusion. "In ict, Daisy Extall, the redhead, was the first of my young ladies o come to mind when you told me what you wanted."

"What about the other?"

"She calls herself Rita Ansell, but that is probably nothing nore than a summer name.* I don't know much about her, but he might be willing. Anyway, I'll put your proposition to them hen they recover."

"Put it to *them*?"

"Of course. The decision they reach will be entirely their wn, and I will not permit any attempt at coercion."

"Have it your own way," Torreson retorted, although such a ourse would never have occurred to him if he had been dealing ith any other madam. "I'll leave getting them, or two more if hey won't, to you. It'll be well worth your while."

"And that of my ladies," Minnie answered, but was pre- ented from continuing by hearing another commotion in the eception room.

This time the sounds instead of being suggestive of feminine onflict, had a masculine timbre. Such screams as were being

"Summer name": A colloquial term for an alias, derived from the conven- on in the Old West that a person could select and employ any name he or he wished. The only permissible way to express doubt or curiosity without viting hostile repercussions was to ask "What is your summer name?" *T.E.*

uttered by the girls registered alarm rather than anger or conflict.

Giving vent to a furious exclamation of "What *now,* for heaven's sake?" Minnie rose and hurried toward the door throug
which she had made her exit last time.

Disregarding the preference expressed by the madam on th
subject of his remaining out of sight, Torreson rose to follow
her.

# 2

# ONE REASON I CAN BEAT
# THEM AT IT

ccupying their usual seats on the porch at either side of the
ont door, the two spotters to whom Victor Torreson had re-
rred were studying a new-looking dark-green 1922 Hudson
uper-Six Coach four-seater passenger car. It was just entering
e open space allocated for the clients of the Premier Chicken
anch to park whatever means of transportation had brought
em there. When they had heard the fight between Rita Ansell
d Daisy Extall start in the reception room, the spotters' atten-
on had been diverted from the vehicle. Nor, as they rose to
vestigate, did they notice that a Pierce-Arrow truck with a
nopy over its back had come to a halt on the road by the
trance of the path leading to the brothel. Being competent in
eir duties, if they had seen the latter, one of them would have
pt it under observation.

There was much justification for Minnie Lassiter's claim that
 raiding party of peace officers could reach her establishment
ithout being detected.

The buildings—a two-story, fair-sized house and a combined

stable and garage—stood in the center of a canyon with hig
and sheer walls. They had the advantage of being in the shade
a grove of cottonwood trees on the banks of a small strea
rising from a natural spring. About a mile in front of the par
ing lot, the entrance to the canyon was some three miles fro
the outskirts of El Paso and off the road—which would becom
known as Highway 80—that turned eastward via Abilene
Fort Worth and Dallas, then across the Louisiana state line
Shreveport.

Behind the property, the canyon narrowed like the neck of
bottle throughout the half a mile separating the buildings fro
the international border formed by the Rio Grande. While
would be possible for raiders to come from that direction, th
terrain was impassable by motor vehicles and their approac
would have to be made on foot or horseback. Nor, as there wa
very little undergrowth in the grove and the trees were we
spaced out, could the arrival be made without being detected b
the staff of the kitchen who acted as lookouts in addition to the
other duties.

A raid by parties from both sides, perhaps supported by mo
officers descending with the aid of ropes down the otherwis
unscalable fifty-foot-high walls of the canyon, could achieve i
purpose of preventing the occupants of the buildings from e
caping. However, because of the effort and risk entailed—whic
would include swimming either up or down the river to arrive
the exit from the canyon—the madam doubted whether such a
operation would ever be carried out. Sheriff Granville Tragg
El Paso County was unlikely to consider the attempt wort
while, or justifiable. Coming from a family that had long bee
connected with the practical enforcement of law and order
Texas,* he accepted that brothels served a useful purpose for th

* As is demonstrated in the Rockaby County series, which covers the duti
performed by and the operations of a present-day sheriff's office, the Trag
family is still involved in the enforcement of law and order in Texas. Som

community as a whole and, with the proviso there were no more serious legal infractions, was willing to allow Minnie to keep operating.

Being all too aware of how swiftly retribution would come if she transgressed against the unofficially official rules that allowed her to remain open under sufferance, Minnie ran the Premier Chicken Ranch with a rod of iron. As it was his organization's most lucrative and steadiest earning brothel, in addition to the feeling he had for her, Hogan Turtle gave her his complete backing. No client—and they could come from any stratum of society, provided they could meet her prices and behaved in the manner she required—had ever been cheated, short-changed, or robbed, in the fashion that frequently brought less well conducted houses into conflict with the law. Nor, except for the occasional unannounced visit such as was being paid by Torreson, did she encourage known criminals on the premises. Certainly none had ever been allowed to hide out there. Knowing this, neither the county sheriff nor the Texas Rangers had seen the need to bother her.

When there had been trouble, which could never be completely avoided in such establishments, the fighting was always restricted to unarmed combat and brought to an end as quickly as possible by Minnie's efficient staff. Furthermore, due to the rules of admittance she imposed and that were rigorously enforced, no knives, firearms, or other weapons, except those in the possession of her employees, were permitted on the premises. The two men seated on the porch as spotters, or their reliefs, were responsible for seeing that the edict regarding the disarmament of the clients was enforced.

Big and brawny, the pair's muscles bulged beneath their brown three-piece suits. As stipulated by the madam, despite

---

details of the careers of two earlier members of the family who served as peace officers in the days of the Old West are given in *Beguinage Is Dead!* and *Set A-Foot. J.T.E.*

the warmth of the afternoon, they had on white shirts with
dark-blue neckties. Bullet-headed, with close-cropped black
hair, their clean-shaven, if blue-chinned and somewhat battered
features showed a strong family resemblance. Although neither
displayed any obvious evidence of being armed, each had a
small bulge in the right side pocket of his jacket. This was
caused by a short, leather-wrapped and spring-loaded sap. If
more effective weapons were required, a twin-barreled, sawed-
off twelve-gauge shotgun was leaning against the right side of
each of their chairs. To the left side of the front door was a large
wooden box into which all the lethal, or potentially dangerous,
devices were placed before their respective owners were allowed
to enter.

"It's Daisy Extall and that gal's arrived last night locking
horns," announced Otis Garnell, the older of the brothers, having crossed to look through the right side window. "And the
new gal's not doing too bad so far. I'd sure like to see her whup
that overstuffed tail peddler good and complete."

"And me," admitted Abel Garnell, duplicating his sibling's
actions on the left. He possessed a similar antipathy—shared by
the majority of the other employees—where the buxom redhead
was concerned. Seeing their employer coming from her office, he
continued regretfully, "It's a mortal shame the new gal won't be
getting the chance to do it now."

"Trust Miz Minnie for that, she surely knows how to stop the
gals when they get to cat-clawing," Otis said, coming to the
same conclusion as his brother. He went on in a more cheerful
tone. "Could be we'll get to find out who-all's the best woman
out of 'em later on, though."

After having watched Minnie bringing the conflict to an end
and seen the removal of the unresisting combatants, the brothers were brought to a remembrance of their duties by hearing
footsteps approaching across the expanse of loose gravel intended to prevent any unheralded arrivals by day or night. Satisfied there was no need for intervention on their part in the

reception room, they swung around to find out who was coming.

Although the Hudson could carry at least four people, only one was in sight. Having walked by the two cars that had delivered the clients already in the building, the driver was almost at the porch by the time the brothers had completed their turns.

On the surface, the newcomer did not present a particularly imposing spectacle. At the most, he was not more than five foot six inches in height. Youthful and bronzed, his clean-shaved face was moderately good-looking without being handsome enough to be eye-catching. A low-crowned, wide-brimmed, black J. B. Stetson hat trailed by its plaited leather *barbiquejo* chin strap on to his shoulders and exposed curly black hair that had been recently trimmed.* He had on a waist-length brown leather jacket that hung unfastened. A tightly rolled scarlet silk bandanna trailed its long ends down the front of an open-necked dark-green satin shirt with a white arrow motif decorating its pockets. A brown waist belt with a fancy buckle and floral patterning cut into its two-and-a-quarter-inch width held up new Levi's pants. Their legs, the cuffs turned back a good three inches, hung outside brown Justin boots carrying Kelly "Petmaker" spurs on their heels.

While the brothers were selected for brawn rather than brains, they had been taught to look beyond external appearances and draw reasonably accurate conclusions about the subjects of their scrutiny. What they saw and deduced from their

* The author suspects that the trend of movies made since the early 1960s to portray cowhands as long-haired and filthy has risen less from the producers' desire for "realism" than because this was the only kind of performers available for supporting roles. In our extensive reference library, we cannot find a dozen photographs of cowboys—as opposed to mountain men, army scouts, or prospectors—who had long hair and bushy beards. In fact, our reading on the subject has led us to assume the term long hair was one of derision and approbrium in the cattle country then as it is today. *J.T.E.*

observations warned them it might be unwise to dismiss the
newly arrived client on account of his lack of size. There was a
good spread to his shoulders, and he tapered down at the waist
in a manner suggesting he might have strength well beyond the
average for one of his height. His face showed little of his
thoughts and his gray eyes met the gaze of the two Garnells
without flinching. If he was paying his first visit to a brothel, he
showed none of the signs of embarrassment or assumed noncha-
lance they had come to expect. Yet, while he was clearly assured
and confident, there was nothing arrogant or self-assertive about
his demeanor. Finally, as far as his eligibility as a client was
concerned, all his clothing looked to have been purchased recently and was of good quality. Nor was the new Hudson, as the
vehicle undoubtedly was, an item that could be bought by a
person who was low on finances.

The newcomer's indications of affluence did not strike either
of the brothers as cause for suspicion. Although there had been
various gloomy predictions of a massive recession when the
world war had come to an end in 1919, this had not material-
ized, and the economy of the United States was still booming in
1924. Despite some alarm on Wall Street due to the exposure of
swindling on a large scale by a dishonest financier, Albert Brickhouse, late the previous year, there had been so sign of the
financial stability decreasing. In fact, even discounting sources
of revenue offered by the ever growing infringements of the Volstead Act, conditions were currently so beneficial that many
people had greater access to wealth than would have been the
case at other times and in different circumstances.

"Howdy you-all, gents," the potential client greeted, his accent that of a Texan who had had a good education. It was firm
in tone but had none of the bombast frequently employed by
men of his height in an attempt to divert attention from their
stature, and it added to the brothers' impression that he was a
person with whom it would be inadvisable to trifle. "I've heard
tell a man can have him a real lively time here."

"You've heard the living truth, mister," Otis confirmed, acting as family spokesman as was usual. While his brother took up a position from which to be able to support him if necessary, he moved forward until he had reached the edge of the porch in front of the door. "But not until *after* he's let me go through him to make sure he's not toting any weapons."

"Well, I'll swan!" the newcomer drawled, his tone still friendly. He halted, apparently completely at his ease. Yet, to the experienced eyes of the brothers, he was as prepared for instant movement as a compressed coil spring as he continued, "Now would that apply to *everybody* who comes?"

*"Everybody* at all, mister," Otis affirmed, speaking politely and firmly, but watching for any warning indication that he was going to meet with a hostile reception. "That's the way Miz Minnie wants it, so *that's* the way it be."

"Time he come a-calling sociablelike, Brother Otis even had to do it to the mayor of El Paso his own self," Abel supported, following his sibling's lead by neither reaching for the sap in his pocket nor doing anything else that could be construed as a threatening gesture. "We *might* just get told to let by the governor of Texas, or good old President Coolridge—except I don't reckon on old Calvin'd be likely to come here—but *nobody* else at all comes through."

"That sounds fair and reasonable enough to me," the newcomer conceded amiably, stepping forward and raising his arms to shoulder height. "Let it never be said's how Rapido Clint wouldn't play the house rules under such conditions. I'll come on up, *amigo,* and, happen you-all don't tickle, you can search right ahead."

Retreating sufficiently to let the apparently compliant visitor join him on the porch, but not so far as to let him get by and reach the door, Otis set about ensuring there would be no infringement of Miz Minnie's regulations for admittance. He worked swiftly and competently. While running his hands along the outstretched arms, he was impressed by the bulk of their biceps and concluded he had not been in error regarding the small young man's muscular development.

The search informed Otis that the newcomer's wallet was thick, but he did not attempt to touch it. Nor did he pay any attention to the handkerchief and loose change which his expertly exploring fingers located in the side pockets of the Levi's. However, finding not so much as a small pocketknife, he asked to see the item that he touched in the right hip pocket but failed to identify. When this was extracted and handed over without the slightest demur, it proved to be a piece of wood about six inches in length. It looked as if it had been cut from the oak handle of a broom. Its ends were rounded and several grooves encircled its middle.

"It's used for playing a game called *yawara,*" Clint explained, in response to an interrogative glance. "I learned to play when I was a button and reckon to be able to beat most folks at it."

"I've never heard of no such game," Otis commented. His brother indicated a similar lack of knowledge.

"There's not many folks around who have," Clint admitted, grinning boyishly as if he was confessing to some mischievous prank. "Which's one reason I can beat them at it."

"Yeah, that being so, I can see's how you-all would be able to," Otis conceded, returning the device. Being satisfied that the newcomer was carrying nothing that could be considered an actual or potentially dangerous weapon, he stepped aside and went on. "Which I reckon I'll stick to things I *know,* like poker or craps. You can go on in, Mr. Clint. Enjoy yourself."

"You-all could maybe teach the gal how to play that you-are-a, whichever way you call it," Abel suggested, also relaxing, confident that the duty assigned to himself and his sibling had been carried out satisfactorily.

"Well, now," Clint replied, tucking the stick back into his right hip pocket. "*That* wasn't *exactly* what I had in mind for doing when I came here."

After the small Texan had disappeared into the building and closed the door behind him, the brothers looked along the trail through the canyon. While the conversation and search had been taking place, the Pierce-Arrow truck had advanced and, just after turning into the entrance, halted again. A tall man whom they assumed to be its driver was peering under its raised hood. Apart from hoping no other customers would come before the vehicle was moved, neither attached any significance to the sight. Provided Minnie's charges were met and her standards of conduct adhered to, there was no restriction placed on the means of transportation by which clients could arrive. In fact, men driving trucks for long distances often called to partake of the excellent free buffet that accompanied the illicit drinks and sexual services of the girls who were available.

Continuing to watch the man, who did not appear to be having any success with whatever mechanical defect had halted the truck in such an inconvenient position, the brothers returned to their chairs. Before they could become settled, they heard noises from the reception room that brought them to their feet. If they had been in less of a hurry to go to investigate, they might have noticed something at the mouth of the canyon to arouse their suspicions.

As soon as the brothers rose and made for the front door, the man they believed to be the driver dropped the truck's hood. However, he ran around to climb into the right side of the cab beside another man who was sitting behind the steering wheel.

# 3

# ARE *YOU-ALL* MAN ENOUGH
# TO STOP ME?

"Gimme another drink, damn it!" demanded the thick-set young man who had supported Daisy Extall in the fight. He crossed to the bar, banged down the glass he had just emptied, and threw a defiant glance at the closed door of Minnie Lassiter's private office.

"Can't rightly do that, Mr. Molyneux," replied the big, brawny middle-aged black man behind the counter, ramming home the cork of the whiskey bottle from which he had been supplying drinks to the speaker's party and the redhead. The gesture and his bearing were redolent of polite yet definite refusal. "Miz Minnie said you-all was to drink up and go."

"I don't take it kind when a goddamned nigger says no to me!" Brian Molyneux warned menacingly, darting glances to the men on either side of him. "Nor to being told what to do by a something cathouse madam, comes to that!"

"Then I reckon the best thing you-all could do'd be leave," the black man stated, his tone hardening without becoming openly truculent.

"And what if *we* don't damn well intend to go?" Molyneux challenged, confident he could count on his two companions to support him. "Just *who's* going to make us?"

"I reckon's how this old sawed-off twelve gauge I'm holding down here might have more than a mite to do with it," the barkeep claimed, having taken his hands from the bottle and lowered them out of sight behind the counter.

"Yeah?" Molyneux answered, but with noticeably less aggression in his bearing and voice. "Well, I'm—"

"Come on, Brian!" Terrence Lacey put in quickly, taking less trouble to conceal his alarm, as he caught hold of the surly-featured young man's right arm. "Let's go. If we make trouble here, they won't have us back."

"And who the hell wants to come *back*?" Molyneux answered, but he allowed himself to be drawn around by his taller, though much lighter, companion with an ease that suggested he was not averse to being persuaded away before he could commit himself to open defiance.

"Yeah, let's scram!" supported the stocky and unprepossessing Jackson Speight, wondering whether there really was a shotgun beneath the counter and yet lacking the courage to put the matter to a test. He shared the other men's conviction that the bartender would be willing to use the weapon, should one be available, so was just as willing to have an excuse to leave. "We can always go to some other place from now on, seeing this is how we get treated here."

Seething with rage over being seen ordered from the premises by the black man, which was how the other occupants of the reception room would consider the departure no matter what he and his companions said, Molyneux shrugged Lacey's hand from his sleeve. However, he hesitated before he turned. A bully by nature and inclination, he hated to be bested at anything and knew that was what had happened.

The sight of Rapido Clint approaching, after he'd hung his Stetson on the rack by the front door, suggested to Molyneux a way by which he could work off some of his anger. Being much less perceptive than the Garnell brothers, he dismissed the newcomer as nothing more than a small and young cowhand—or employed in some even less important capacity on a ranch—clad in go-to-town clothes. He felt sure he would not encounter any serious resistance in that direction. There might even, he realized, be a chance of extracting revenge upon the man behind the counter while he was relieving his ruffled feelings.

"Hey, short stuff!" Molyneux called with a sneer, after having darted a pointed glance from Speight to the bottle of whiskey and on to the barkeep, and receiving a nod from his companion to show his meaning had been understood. Striding toward the new arrival while speaking, he continued. "Are you *old* enough to be in a place like this?"

"Well, now," Clint replied, halting to stand in the same way as he had when addressed by Otis Garnell on his arrival at the Premier Chicken Ranch. But this time his tone was filled with what his challenger took to be tremulous defiance. "Are *you-all* man enough to stop me coming in?"

"Hot damn!" Molyneux spat out, wondering whether the small Texan was relying on obtaining support from the three cowhands who were already present. Concluding their intervention would offer opportunities to do damage to the reception room, he went on. "You'll soon see I am!"

As he delivered the threat, the big man lunged forward. As he did so, reaching toward his intended victim with both hands—he saw no need to employ a more scientific kind of attack—something strange happened.

Suddenly and inexplicably, as far as Molyneux was concerned, the "youngster" seemed not only to have grown older but to have stopped looking small and harmlessly insignificant.

Such was the strength of Clint's personality, in fact, that he now conveyed the impression of having become larger than his would-be assailant!

Nor did the Texan restrict himself to merely disconcerting Molyneux.

Moving with an alacrity that demonstrated how he could have acquired the sobriquet "Rapido"—a border Mexican colloquialism meaning *"very* fast"—Clint glided to meet the approaching man.

Just what happened next, neither Molyneux nor any of the onlookers could later describe with certainty. All he knew and they saw was that the small Texan caught his right wrist in both hands, pivoted clear of him, and gave a twisting pull on it in some way. An instant later the burly man felt his feet leaving the floor. Turning a half somersault, he alighted on his back. Yet, fortunately for him, he landed before he could start to comprehend what was happening and try to break his fall. As a result, he came down with his body relaxed. While the impact hurt, the result was much less severe than might otherwise have been the case. Some of the breath was knocked from his body, but he avoided being knocked out.

"Come on, Terry!" Speight shouted, startled by seeing Molyneux thrown to the floor with such apparent ease, but recovering his wits quickly. "Let's get the goddamned son of a bitch!"

"Let's do just that!" Lacey agreed, thrusting himself away from the counter and expecting his companion to accompany him.

Such was not Speight's immediate intention.

"Hey!" the bartender exclaimed, jolted out of the surprised condition he had entered while watching the way in which Clint had dealt with Molyneux. He brought his hands into view involuntarily, showing them to be empty. "Quit that, y—"

On seeing that the bartender had been bluffing about the shotgun, Speight had no further qualms over doing what he had deduced Molyneux expected of him. As he was snatching up the bottle of whiskey, however, one of the girls screamed a warning. Goaded by fear of the consequences if he failed, Speight hurled the missile across the counter. For a disturbing moment, seeing the burly black man begin to duck, he thought he had missed. While he came near to doing so, the result served his purpose. While the bottle struck only a glancing blow, which caused it to ricochet from the victim's skull instead of shattering, the force was nevertheless sufficient to stun him. He collapsed to disappear behind the bar.

After coming up behind Clint, who had turned and was looking down at Molyneux, Lacey encircled and pinned his arms to his sides. The intention was to hold him immobile and leave Speight at liberty to avenge their companion's discomfiture.

The slim young man received a shock.

Having been laboring under a similar misapprehension as Molyneux regarding the small Texan (or he would not have taken the chance of attacking), Lacey had not been subjected to the sight of Rapido's apparent metamorphosis, and he did not envision any great difficulty in keeping his captive under control. To his horror, he found his grip was being broken with a speed and force that threw his arms apart and left him open for reprisals, which were not long in coming. Almost immediately, in fact, an elbow rammed into his solar plexus and caused him to back away, emitting a croak of pain.

Not far enough, however!

After spinning around swiftly, the small Texan delivered a backhand slap to the side of Lacey's head. It sent him spinning across the room until he collided with the bar. Hanging there somewhat dazed, the only consolation he could draw was that his actions had allowed Speight to gain an advantage. Feeling certain this would permit him to take over the part he had expected his cohort to carry out when grabbing Molyneux's attacker, he pushed himself forward to administer the intended beating.

Satisfied that his slender companion was at least diverting Clint's attention, Speight was advancing to lend a hand when the release was effected. Ignoring the continuing shrieks of alarm and protest from the girls, apart from noticing that they were restraining the other three cowhands from intervening, he watched Lacey being knocked aside and made the most he could of the adversely changed conditions. Closing in fast, he threw his left arm around the small Texan's neck and obtained a headlock.

Bent forward at the waist and trapped, Clint did not attempt to escape by sheer strength as he had from Lacey's much weaker reverse bear hug. Instead, while putting up sufficient of struggle to make his captor interlace the fingers and employ both arms to retain the hold, he reached behind him with his right hand. After removing the small piece of wood from his right hip pocket, he grasped it so the ends were protruding on either side of his clenched fist.

In spite of the explanation he had given to the Garnell brothers, leading them to assume it was a completely innocuous toy, Clint showed that the device had qualities neither had suspected. In fact, as he jabbed the rounded end ahead of his thumb and forefinger into the kidney region of his assailant's back, it proved to be a most effective if unconventional weapon. A croak of agony burst from Speight as the blow was struck. Arching his spine and releasing his hold, he staggered forward with his hands going involuntarily to the point of impact.

Seeing Lacey was once more coming in his direction and Molyneux was starting to sit up, Clint put a foot against the seat of Speight's trousers and shoved. Propelled across the room with no control over his limbs, the stocky man caused two of the shrieking girls to jump aside. After passing heedlessly between them, he sprawled facedown across an unoccupied table.

Coming into range while the small Texan was returning the foot to the floor, Lacey elected to display his skill as a boxer. Bringing up his clenched fists, he began to essay what should have been a classic one-two attack. However, neither the right cross he launched nor the left hook with which he intended to follow it up achieved any success. In fact, the latter blow was never even begun.

Swinging around his stick-filled fist with the speed and accuracy of a striking diamondback rattlesnake, Clint caught the inside of Lacey's right forearm with the end that was protruding. Even as the punch was being deflected in a most painful way, the device reversed its course almost without appearing to need any guidance on his part. Rising and descending extremely rapidly, the same end impacted against the cocked left wrist to produce an equally painful effect.

Whimpering in torment and with his arms flopping limply to his sides, Lacey turned to reel away from his assailant. Once again his retreat proved to be neither fast nor far enough for safety. Rising on his left foot just as the front and interior door —the latter marked "PRIVATE No Admittance"—were thrown open with equal violence, Clint jumped to send the sole of his right boot in a circular motion that delivered a thrusting kick to the center of the slender young man's back. Swiftly performed though the movement had been, the result was hard enough to throw its recipient in a helpless run toward the second door.

Upon entering the reception room hurriedly from her office, Minnie Lassiter took in the scene and could hardly credit the evidence of her eyes. While she had surmised correctly who was involved in the disturbance, she found that her further summation was erroneous. The three cowhands who had been present when she entered to end the fight between the two girls were not participants. However, on turning her gaze to what was obviously the only other antagonist in the fracas, she was startled by the discovery that he alone was responsible for the trio's condition.

Not that the madam was allowed to ponder upon the matter for more than a moment.

The haste with which Minnie had left the office was carrying her into danger.

Seeing a vague shape ahead of him, the tears caused by the pain he was experiencing blurred his vision and prevented Lacey from making any identification. So he acted as a result of a fear-inspired instinct. Without pausing to think how the *big* Texan could have arrived in such a position, but believing that it was he who stood before him, Lacey raised his throbbing arms with the intention of launching an attack. It was, as any of the brothel's employees could have warned him, far from the most judicious action of his life.

Stopping in her tracks at the first intimation of danger, Minnie knew just how best to deal with the situation. Inclining her torso rearward, she brought up her right foot in a swiftly flowing and graceful yet *very* purposeful swinging motion. This caused the bell-bottomed legs of the pajamas' trousers to ride back and exposed the white ballet dancer's slippers she always wore at the Premier Chicken Ranch. Passing between Lacey's outstretched hands before they could reach their objective, the hard-packed resinous filling of the right point caught him beneath the chin. Such was the force behind the rapidly delivered kick that, although his feet continued to advance, the upper portion of his body was tilted to the rear. Going down, he did not feel the impact as he crashed supine and unconscious to the floor.

Arriving on the scene at almost the same time as their employer, the Garnell brothers were not quite as taken aback by what they saw. Having made Clint's acquaintance on his arrival, they had formed the impression that his physical appearance was deceiving. For all that, they were surprised by the evidence of his success in dealing with three larger and heavier men in such a short period. Practical experience in such matters suggested that, having failed to draw the correct conclusions, the trio had been taken unawares by their apparently diminutive and harmless victim. However, the pair did not allow their speculations to divert them from what they knew to be their duty.

Being so engrossed in the sights that had greeted them and in what they were about to do, the brothers paid no more attention than any other occupant of the room to the sound of a rapidly approaching vehicle. Instead, taking the saps from their pockets, they strode purposely forward on diverging courses.

Going to where Molyneux was trying to get up, Otis brought the attempt to an end with a careful blow from the leather-wrapped device he was holding. As the burly young trouble-maker was collapsing, Speight—who was rolling erect from the table across which he had fallen—received similar treatment at Abel's hands and also went down.

Such was the skill of the brothers that they stunned and rendered their respective victims innocuous, but inflicted no serious injury.

"What the hell kind of crummy trap is *this*?" Clint demanded loudly, glaring around. Yet, strangely, considering that he appeared to be bristling with indignation, he returned the short stick that had proved to be such an effective weapon to his right hip pocket while speaking. "I hadn't even got to the goddamned bar before I was jumped by those three mother-something sons of bitches, and not one lousy bastard as much's lifted a finger to help me take them out."

Which, although nobody offered to mention the matter, was definitely *not* a suitable tone and manner for a person who had been involved in a fight at the Premier Chicken Ranch to adopt. However, in spite of showing resentment over the comment, not one of the clients or employees made any response. Catching the madam's eye and receiving a prohibitive shake from her head, even the Garnell brothers made no attempt to advance and remonstrate with the insulting young man. Nor, because of their complete absorption in what was happening, did they give any thought to the sounds that suggested a heavy vehicle was approaching the front of the building instead of halting in the parking lot.

"Didn't they?" Minnie asked, walking past the motionless figure on the floor without giving it so much as a glance. Holding out her right hand, she went on in a tone that was almost amiable. "Then, as owner of the Premier Chicken Ranch, let me offer my apologies for the way you've been treated."

Annoyed by the small Texan's behavior and having a rule about the treatment accorded to every participant of a fight on the premises, the madam intended to inflict the penalty personally. She could have left the task in the capable hands of the Garnell brothers, but the circumstances suggested that to do so might provoke further trouble. The small newcomer's attire indicated he could be a cowhand. While the other three members of that close-knit fraternity had not offered to assist him against his former assailants and showed signs of disapproving of his disrespectful comments, they might decide to lend him a hand if they saw him in difficulties while under attack by her larger and heavier men. Past experience led Minnie to believe they would be less likely to intervene with her as the inflictor of the punishment.

When Clint accepted her hand, Minnie gripped his tightly and pulled with the intention of kneeing him in the groin.

# 4

# THAT MEANS *YOU* MORE THAN ANYBODY, RAPIDO CLINT!

The trick Minnie Lassiter was employing had long been her favorite means of dealing with recalcitrant or obstreperous clients. It had never failed in the past.

Caught unexpectedly with the somewhat bony knee—powered by a slender leg, which nevertheless had muscles like steel springs—in the most vulnerable portion of the masculine anatomy, every man who had been subjected to a similar attack invariably subsided helplessly at the madam's feet.

On this occasion, however, the desired result did not come about.

Instead of allowing himself to be jerked forward on to Minnie's rising left knee, Rapido Clint braced himself against the pull. Remaining on the spot, he returned the tug with one that was even more vigorous. As he did so, he twisted himself away at the hips and caused the knee to land in a far less dangerous fashion than was intended on his hip. Before the bent limb could be withdrawn, he hooked his left hand underneath it. Giving an upward heave, he shoved hard with his right hand. Releasing both his holds simultaneously, surprise having caused the madam to relax her grip, he sent her staggering away from him. In spite of her desperate efforts to regain her equilibrium, it was destroyed and she tripped to sit painfully on her rump.

"Hey!" Otis Garnell bellowed indignantly, startled by seeing his employer's hitherto successful tactics brought to nothing in such a fashion. The sight also prevented him from turning at the sound of a vehicle being brought to a brake-squealing halt in front of and close to the Premier Chicken Ranch. "You can't treat Miz Minnie that ways!"

"God blast you!" Abel Garnell was shouting at the same moment, equally infuriated by the way in which the madam had been treated and also losing his former goodwill toward the small Texan. He too was so incensed that he was ignoring something that should have demanded the instant attention of himself and his sibling. "I'll fix you for that!"

"Try it *any* time!" Clint offered loudly, backing toward the counter and holding his empty hands in a position of readiness.

Even as the brothers were starting to move forward, their saps grasped for use in avenging the affront to their well-liked employer, heavy footsteps pounded rapidly across the front porch. Although Otis and Abel began to turn around, they were too late to do anything. Nor, even if they had been inclined to do so, would the opportunity have been granted to them.

Each holding either a Winchester 1894 model or an 1897 model trench gun* manufactured by the same company ready for use, although the latter were not fitted with their bayonets, four men burst through the front door in rapid succession. On

---

* "Trench gun": A five-shot, tubular-magazine, pump-action, twelve-gauge shotgun designed for use in the trench warfare of World War I. The twenty-inch-long barrel had a radiating cooling sleeve and was equipped to take a bayonet. It was an extremely effective close-quarters' weapon, particularly when loaded with buckshot. *J.T.E.*

crossing the threshold of the reception room, they fanned out so
not one of them was impeding any of the others' line of fire.

The smooth way in which the men had entered came as no
surprise to the other occupants of the room. A silver badge,
comprised of a five-pointed star in a circle, was pinned to the
left breast of each newcomer's shirt. Madam, employees, and
clients were alike in recognizing the insignia of the Texas Rangers. They were aware of that organization's long tradition where
the handling of firearms was concerned, so they knew its members could be counted on to be well versed in how to behave in
such circumstances.

"Stay put, all of you!" commanded the big, burly, blond man
in the lead, making an all-embracing gesture with his trench gun
to emphasize the words. He wore the attire of a working cowhand and had a Colt Government 1911 model .45 automatic
pistol tucked butt forward into the left side of his waist belt to
augment a similar weapon in the holster on his right thigh. Like
his rugged, reddened rather than tanned features, his Texas
drawl held a distinct suggestion of Germanic origins. "Rangers
here!"

"That means *you* more than anybody, Rapido Clint!" warned
the officer on the left, directing the barrel of his carbine at the
small Texan. Tall, slender yet wiry, he was swarthily handsome.
He had on a white straw boater hat, an open-necked white
sharkskin shirt with a multicolored silk cravat, gray flannels,
and mottled alligator-hide shoes. For all his dapper dress, he too
wore a gunbelt with a Colt automatic pistol in its holster. He
spoke with a slight Gallic accent and continued, sounding almost cheerful, "It's *you* we've come after, *mon ami!*"

"And it's a pity that goddamned half-breed sidekick of yours
isn't here as well," the man on the right declared, also covering
the small Texan with the Winchester he held. Only just over
medium height, almost as broad as he was tall, he was dressed
after the fashion of a Mexican *vaquero* and had such a villainous

cast of heavily mustached, olive-skinned features, even his mother might have been excused if she had taken a dislike to his appearance. In fact, he looked more like the popular conception of a *bandido* than a member of an honorable and respected law enforcement organization. His English was good but supplied a hint of his Hispanic birthright, and he too carried a sidearm. "That way we'd have the pair of you to take so as the hangman at the Walls* would have you stretching hemp!"

Although he had set out to follow Minnie Lassiter from the office, Victor Torreson had changed his mind while still inside. He had concluded that such a blatant disregard for her wishes would not be well received and might even put in jeopardy the assignment he had been sent across the Rio Grande to carry out. Knowing that the man upon whom he depended for being allowed to remain in Mexico—and therefore beyond the reach of the law in the United States—would be furious if he failed in his task, he had halted instead of going through the door. But he watched from inside the doorway to see what was going on.

When he saw the Texas Rangers, the New York fugitive was grateful that he had been so cautious. Deciding that they were fully occupied by keeping the occupants of the reception room under observation and might be unaware of his presence, he carefully closed the door. Letting out a sigh of relief when he had accomplished this without being challenged, he crossed swiftly to the desk. After picking up and donning his *sombrero,* he went to the exit from the office that would allow him to emerge on the left side of the main building. His horse was in the combined stable and garage at the rear of the property. Once mounted, he could ride south along the canyon and, by crossing the Rio Grande, reach the safety of Mexican soil.

When he opened the door and peered warily out, Torreson

* "The Walls": The main state penitentiary in Huntsville, Walker County, Texas. *J.T.E.*

saw nothing to alarm him. Filled with a comforting conviction that his presence had not been detected by the Rangers and satisfied that the entire raiding party was inside the building, he stepped out. Wondering why the peace officers had decided to pull a raid at such an inopportune moment, he began to walk toward the stable.

Before the fugitive had reached the end of the building, a menacing snarl and the patter of rapidly approaching feet diverted his thoughts from which of the rubes might have been the Rangers' objective. After glancing over his shoulder, he swung around rapidly. Then he froze as if suddenly turned to stone. In spite of his protests, he had been compelled to leave his revolver in the custody of the Garnell brothers on his arrival like every other client. However, even if it had been in the spring-retention shoulder holster beneath the left side of his *bolero* jacket, he would not have attempted to draw it. His every instinct warned him that to do anything other than stand perfectly still would be more than the height of folly. It could lead to him sustaining a serious injury.

The blood-curdling growl was emanating from a large and powerful-looking dog, which came loping swiftly toward the New Yorker. Although he guessed it was a hound of some kind, and although circumstances had caused him to become a moderately competent horseman, his lack of interest in other bucolic pursuits and pastimes prevented him from making any closer identification.

To a person with a more extensive knowledge of such matters, the dark bluish-gray coloration, liberally bespeckled with numerous irregularly shaped black spots, the black head and saddle indicated it was a bluetick coonhound—albeit one bred specifically for hunting big game such as cougar, jaguar, black and grizzly bears, rather than smallish, semiarboreal creatures like raccoon and opossum—and an exceptionally fine example of the breed.*

There was, however, more than the implied threat of the bluetick—serious though that was—to make Torreson see the futility of resistance or flight.

A tall man was ambling after the dog in a leisurely seeming fashion that nevertheless covered plenty of ground surprisingly quickly. Lean as a steer raised in the greasewood country, apart from a suggestion that he could be well on in years, his leathery brown features gave little indication of his actual age. Although at that moment his face was set in grimly determined lines, the wrinkles at the corners of his keen blue eyes and the narrow slash of a mouth were suggestive of a dry sense of humor. He had on a battered and ancient-looking grayish-green Stetson that had started its life white, a somewhat baggy brown coat, blue shirt buttoned to the collar, but without a necktie, Levi's pants, and black Justin boots. Like his headdress, both the latter items of attire appeared old enough to have been part of the original consignments put on the market by their respective manufacturers.** While he was not carrying either a carbine or a trench gun, an ivory-butted Colt Civilian model Frontier revolver dangled, almost negligently it seemed, in his right hand, the four-and-three-quarters-inch-long barrel pointing at the

* Information regarding various breeds of hounds used for hunting big game animals is given in *Hound Dog Man* and, to a lesser extent, *Sidewinder*. A more detailed description of this particular bluetick coonhound can be found in Case One, "Alvin Fog's Mistake," *You're a Texas Ranger, Alvin Fog. J.T.E.*

** Levi's were first designed and manufactured by Levi Strauss in San Francisco, California, in 1850. Justin boots were first made by Joseph Justin in 1879, at Ole Spanish Fort, on the Texas side of the Red River. Along with those of Colt, Winchester, and Stetson, the excellence of these two manufacturers' products gained such popularity that their names have become famous throughout the world. *J.T.E.*

ground.* The badge of a Texas Ranger glinted dully in the sun from the left breast of his shirt.

Instead of coming close enough to be kicked, should Torreson have been contemplating making such an attempt, the bluetick halted in front of him just beyond the range of his legs. It was, on the other hand, near enough to launch an immediate attack if the need arose. What was more, it conveyed the impression of eagerly awaiting the slightest opportunity to do so. A ridge of hair bristled along its back and, as stiff as a poker, its tail was carried high in a forward-pointing crescent. Although it was no longer making any sound, its *very* impressive mouthful of teeth were being displayed in a lip-curling if silent snarl. It looked as dangerous as a winter-starved grizzly bear fresh out of hibernation, and its demeanor was sufficient to scare a city dweller, with little experience of such things, into immobility even without the support offered by the elderly man who was approaching.

Silently cursing the adverse turn taken by his fortunes, the New Yorker kept his head lowered. He hoped that the wide and circular brim of his *sombrero* would throw such a dark shadow over his face that he would escape recognition. Or that the old man, who did not strike him as being particularly bright and efficient, would fail to identify him. In the latter case, perhaps aided by a judicious bribe, he might be able to bluff the peace officer into believing he was no more than a harmless citizen whose career could be ruined should he be arrested during a raid on a place like the Premier Chicken Ranch.

Neither hope came to fruition.

"Well, if I'll not be 'ternally damnation-ified, which I've been told right frequent' is going to happen," the elderly Ranger de-

* The Frontier is the name given to a Colt Model P "Peacemaker" chambered to take a .44-40-.44 of an inch caliber, with a forty-grain charge of black powder—bullet, permitting the same ammunition to be used in the revolver and the Winchester 1873 model rifle or carbine. Further details regarding the various types and barrel lengths the Model P—first made in 1873—can be found in the Floating Outfit series. *J.T.E.*

clared, stopping a short distance from the criminal. "If this just ain't your for-tune-ate-ical day, Jubal Branch. Hey, what do you-all reckon, Lightning? We'n's've done gone and caught us Mr. Victor Torreson of li'l ole New York City, his own self."

"You—you're badly mistaken, Officer!" the fugitive contradicted, trying to make his voice sound anything except like a person born and raised in New York. "I'm A. J. Harper from Kansas City, Miss—"

"Now you-all wouldn't be trying to shit a poor, un-eddicated li'l ole country-boy shitter like me, would you, Victor?" Sergeant Jubal Branch interrupted in a mildly chiding tone. " 'Cause you-all don't sound *nothing* like somebody from Missouri. Tell you, though. Should it come out's I'm doing you-all an in-just-ical, I'll up and a-polly-gerate most humble. But, until that eventualates, just you put your hands behind your back and, good manners or not, turn it to me."

"What for?" the New Yorker challenged, still trying to sound like a righteously indignant and innocent taxpayer.

"Could be that I just don't take kind to the look of your face," Branch explained, his lazy Texas drawl sardonic, as he removed a set of handcuffs from the left side pocket of his jacket. His voice retained its bantering, yet somehow also threatening timbre as he continued. "I'd do it real *pronto*, was I you-all, 'case ole Lightning there takes a miss-like to it same's me. He's sort of apt to start showing his miss-likings fast and *real* painful."

"You've no right to do *this*!" Torreson protested, accepting there was no chance of persuading the elderly sergeant that a mistake in identity was being made and doing as he had been instructed. "I'm a naturalized Mexican citizen now."

"So I've heard tell," Branch conceded, but showed not the slightest sign of alarm over the implied threat of possible international repercussions. "Trouble being's far's that goes, Mexico comes to a right sudden stop halfway across that ole river down the canyon a smidgin. So you're on the sacred soil of the great and sovereign State of Texas. Which, seeing's how we let the Yankees join up with us back in forty-six,* we're a real *big* part of the United States of America and it's our bounden, legal-sworn duty to pick up 'n' return all wanted miss-cree-aunts to who-all's wanting 'em back. And, mister, way I hear tell, the New York Police Deep-heart-ment wants you-all back just's bad as all get-out."

While speaking, the elderly sergeant had advanced and deftly attached the handcuffs to the fugitive's wrists. The task required the employment of both hands, meaning that the revolver had had to be disposed of in some fashion. Despite appreciating the point, Torreson did not even start to consider trying to take advantage of what might have appeared to be an opportunity. As he was turning his back on his captor, the bluetick had circled and halted in front of him in another position from which he could be kept under unimpeded observation, or attacked if he tried anything.

"How well do they pay you for sending their fugitives back to them?" Torreson asked, having obeyed after the handcuffing was completed and his captor ordered him to turn around, hating the feel of the cold steel on his wrists.

"Nothing," Branch admitted. "Less there's a ree-ward offered, that is."

"Is there one offered for *me*?"

"Not so far's I know. But doing a service for a brother peace officer goes with the badge, they do say."

"Only doing a service doesn't make a man rich," Torreson remarked, believing he had heard a wistful and regretful tone in the elderly sergeant's voice.

---

* On February 16, 1846, following protracted negotiations, the United States of America annexed the vast territory that was then the Republic of Texas. The population had established the republic following the campaign that culminated, on April 21, 1836, in the decisive Battle of San Jacinto. An account of some events that immediately preceded the battle is given in *Ole Devil at San Jacinto. J.T.E.*

"And letting you-all *go* would?" Branch asked.

"It'd help," the New Yorker declared, wondering if the five hundred dollars in his wallet would be a sufficiently large bribe to obtain his freedom.

"That sounds almost like you're making li'l ole me a proper-sitty-on," the sergeant remarked. "Which I hope for your sake you're *not*. A man with a rape and four murders hanging 'round his neck shouldn't go making things no worse by additionaling trying to bribe a duly appointed 'n' legally swored-in officer of the law to his sins. Let's go inside."

"Who the hell snitched?" the fugitive demanded furiously, instead of doing as he had been told.

"Who on?" Branch inquired innocently if ungrammatically.

"Me!"

"You?"

"Who the something hell do you think I meant?"

"Can't say's I'm a whole heap tooken with such language, young feller," Branch reproved mildly. "But I conclude, being a big city boy 'n' all, you likely don't know no better. Anyways, it wasn't *you-all'* s we come looking for." Cocking his head toward the building and listening for a moment, he went on. "Don't hear no ruckus nor shooting in there. So it looks like the boys must've took him un-awary-like."

"Took *who*?" Torreson wanted to know, although thinking that—unlikely as he might appear to be on the surface—only one of the rubes he had seen in the reception room seemed to warrant the attention of so many Rangers.

"Ornery young cuss name of Rapido Clint," Branch explained, confirming the fugitive's supposition. "He's bad wanted up to Cowtown,* 'mong other places. Only, him being such a short-growed young son of a bitch, what we've been told about

---

* "Cowtown": A colloquial name for Fort Worth, Tarrant County, Texas. *J.T.E.*

him, you'd never think it of him first sight took. Let's you 'n' me go on in and see if the boys've put the arm on him, shall we?"

"Call off that goddamned mutt first!" Torreson requested nervously, being unable to see the dog as it had not followed him around as he turned to speak to the elderly peace officer.

"Who, ole Lightning?" Branch asked, sounding surprised by the suggestion. "Why, he wouldn't go hurting *nobody*!"

Scowling in malevolent disbelief, the fugitive from New York glanced slowly and cautiously over his shoulder. The sight that met his gaze was so unexpected that, for a moment, he wondered whether his eyes were playing tricks on him. No longer did the big bluetick look menacing, or even alert. It was sprawling in an ungainly fashion on the ground and appeared to have fallen asleep. As he began to walk hesitantly toward the side door, it hauled itself erect slowly and with a suggestion of nearly uncontrollable weariness. Nor did it display any greater sign of vitality as, with what sounded like a sigh of protest at being forced into such unnecessary activity, it followed them into the building.

# 5

# THERE'S NO WAY RAPE
# CAN HAPPEN

"Howdy you-all, Miz Minnie," Sergeant Jubal Branch greeted respectfully, sweeping off his decrepit-looking Stetson to exhibit short and grizzled grayish-brown hair, as he came from the office behind Victor Torreson with the big bluetick slouching on his heels as if close to exhaustion. While speaking, he strolled to where the madam of the Premier Chicken Ranch stood massaging her pajama-covered rump and glowering at Rapido Clint. "Right sorry us good old boys had to come a-busting in on you-all without checking our weapons with Otis 'n' Abel there. We would've, mind, only we're here on awf-ish-ee-yawl biz-ernesses and not for pleasure-ables."

While delivering his apologetic explanation, the elderly peace officer was also looking around the reception room. His keen-eyed scrutiny took everything in, but his leathery features gave not the slightest indication of how he regarded what he was seeing. His gaze rested for a moment on where the black bartender, still glassy-eyed and looking dazed, had risen and was leaning for support against the counter. Then it passed, without

eliciting any comment from him, to the three unconscious troublemakers. Although he drew the correct conclusions when he
saw the Garnell brothers, holding their saps, hovering over
Brian Molyneux and Jackson Speight, he made no reference to
them. Nor, apparently, did he pay any greater attention to the
three clearly perturbed young cowhands and the girls who were
standing in postures of alarm. Instead, he brought his examination to an end when it reached the small Texan. Despite the
latter's wrists being secured in front of him by handcuffs, the
thick-set Chicano\* and burly Germanic Texas Rangers were
covering him with their Winchester carbine and trench gun.
Both appeared tense and were clearly taking no chances.

"I appreciate the distinction, Sergeant Branch, although I
can't say I *approve* of having my guests and young ladies startled by such a boisterous arrival," Minnie Lassiter replied,
adopting the "grand dame" posture and tone she used so well.
Then her gaze turned to Torreson and she continued in tones
redolent of surprise. "Why, merciful heavens above! Whatever
has Mr. Smethurst done?"

"Told you-all a mite of a miss-truth when he said he was Mr.
Smethurst, for one thing, Miz Minnie," Branch answered, with
such apparent sincerity that he might have believed the madam
was not aware of his prisoner's true identity. "Truth being,
though, we'n's only come here after that young jasper's Carlos
'n' Dutchy're watching over so carefullike. Only, coming on this
longhorn a-sneaking suspish-ical-looking out of your office
when I knowed you wouldn't be in it, I concluded I'd best ask
him if you-all knowed he was in there. When I stopped him,
dog-my-cats if I didn't reck-hog-nerize him's being bad wanted
by the New York Police Deep-heart-ment. So I just natural' up
and brought him back with me. You know he was in your office?"

---

\* "Chicano": A Mexican born, or residing, in the United States of America. *J.T.E.*

"Yes, he came to ask if I would accept his check, and the commotion in here brought me out before I could reply," Minnie replied, so smoothly and without hesitation she might have been speaking the truth. Wanting to avoid being questioned any further on the matter, the throbbing in her rump suggested a way by which she might be able to divert attention from it. It also had the added inducement of allowing her to take revenge for the humiliation she had suffered. Leaving Branch, she walked toward the small Texan and went on, almost mildly, "So *you* are the reason for all *this*?"

As she finished speaking, having gauged the distance accurately with her eyes, the madam whipped her right leg upward. Except for the slight yet noticeable emphasis she had placed on the words you and this, there had been nothing in her demeanor to offer the slightest warning of her intentions. Delivered at great speed and with the deadly precision of one well versed in the French style of foot-and-fist boxing known as *savate,* in which she had become interested when reading of how it had been used to very good effect by her girlhood heroine, Belle "the Rebel Spy" Boyd,* the intended attack should have attained the success that similar tactics had invariably achieved in the past.

Once again, Rapido Clint proved to be the exception.

Stepping backward a long and rapid pace, the small Texan carried himself beyond the reach of the rising ballet slipper. Nor did his evasion end there. Bringing up his arms, he demonstrated that having his wrists manacled did not deny him the use of his hands by catching Minnie's ankle in them. A startled

* Some details of the career of Belle "the Rebel Spy" Boyd can be read in: *The Colt and the Saber, The Rebel Spy, The Bloody Border, Back to the Bloody Border* (Berkley Medallion Books, 1978 edition retitled, *Renegade*), *The Hooded Riders, The Bad Bunch,* Part Eight, "Affair Of Honor," *J.T.'s Hundredth, To Arms! To Arms! In Dixie! The South Will Rise Again, The Nighthawk, The Quest for Bowie's Blade, The Remittance Kid, The Whip and the War Lance,* and Part Five, "The Butcher's Fiery End," *J.T.'s Ladies. J.T.E.*

and infuriated squeal burst from her as she was given a swinging jerk that caused her to twirl helplessly on her left foot. Then, in a motion similar to when he had been completing Jackson Speight's discomfiture, Clint placed his right foot on her already sore rump and gave it a sharp thrust. Driven forward with arms flailing wildly, her progress was halted by her collision with two of the girls. Unlike their companions when Speight had been treated in the same manner, they made no attempt to avoid her. Fortunately, they were sufficiently large and strong to withstand the impact, and they contrived to keep her in an upright posture.

"You goddamned bastard!" bellowed the burly blond Ranger, his tone becoming more noticeably Germanic, leaping forward and swinging his left arm in a horizontal arc before anybody else could move. "Treat Miz Minnie like that, will you?"

Apparently the big peace officer's speed and wrathful indignation caused him to strike with less accuracy than might otherwise have been the case. Instead of the fist landing on the small Texan's head, the forearm caught his shoulder. For all that, the force of the blow sent him staggering across the room. He tripped and, as he went down, showed the agility of an exceptionally competent horseman by landing and rolling until being brought to a halt against the wall. However, it seemed his misfortunes were not at an end. Spitting out curses in German as well as English, his burly assailant lumbered after him swiftly and purposefully.

"Just you-all hold hard there for a dad-blasted minute, Dutchy!" Branch bellowed, moving forward more rapidly than usual as the Teutonic peace officer came to a halt and drew back his foot for a kick. "We're having none of *that* kind of thing here!"

"Who the hell says so?" challenged Hans "Dutchy"

Soehnen,* glowering over his shoulder, but he refrained from completing the attack.

"I reckon's you might say's I do," the elderly sergeant answered, continuing to advance in a grimly determined manner. "You-all can't go miss-ree-treating no prisoner when you're riding in *my* posse. Not with this many witter-nessers on hand, anyways." Coming to a halt, he swung his gaze to where the madam was shrugging herself free from the restraint of the two girls. Knowing her of old, he went on. "Which same goes for you-all, Miz Minnie, so you just haul in your horns and leave be."

"Whatever you say, Sergeant Branch!" the madam asserted, but if looks could have killed, the small Texan would have died on the spot.

*"Gracias,* old-timer," Clint drawled, struggling to his feet.

*"Old-timer?"* Branch repeated in an indignation-filled bellow. "Danged if you-all ain't just fit to make a man start wishing there wasn't so many witter-nessers to hand. Where-at's that nogood sidekick of your'n?"

"Gone over to the *Pehnane* Comanch' reservation,"** the small Texan replied. "Allowed he wanted to visit a spell with his kinfolks and say Howdy, you-all to some of those pretty li'l Injun gals."

"You just stay put there, Mr. Torreson!" Branch commanded over his shoulder, before continuing to question the second prisoner. "So he's not likely to be coming here, huh?"

The comment to the New York fugitive had been elicited by the elderly sergeant having heard a significant sound from his rear.

---

* In Texas, a man of Teutonic appearance was frequently called "Dutchy" even though his origins had been in Germany and not the Netherlands. *J.T.E.*
** How the *Pehnane*—Wasp, Quick Stinger, or Raider—band of the Comanche nation was persuaded to go on to the reservation is told in *Sidewinder. J.T.E.*

Noticing that everybody else's attention was directed toward the other side of the room, Torreson decided to take advantage of the opportunity with which he believed he was being presented. The big bluetick had collapsed on its side and, from all appearances, had fallen asleep the moment its master had begun to address the madam. However, as soon as the fugitive made a movement, it came to its feet in a far from lethargic fashion. The menacing growl that rumbled from its throat was sufficient to make him change his mind even before Branch delivered the order. Nor did he think of making another attempt at flight when, on his having ceased moving, the dog resumed its attitude of somnolence.

"I wouldn't reckon so," Clint declared. "Ole Comanch' doesn't go a whole heap for the notion of having to pay for *it.*"

"He'd sooner rape for it, huh?" Soehnen suggested coldly.

"According to some old Chinese jasper I've read about, there's no way rape can happen," the small Texan pointed out in a mocking tone. "On account of that a gal with her skirt hoisted up should be able to run a whole heap faster than a feller with his pants around his knees. Which that li'l German gal—"

"You lousy bastard!" Soehnen spat out furiously, swinging up his trench gun in both hands with the intention of using its butt as a club.

"You hold off there, Dutchy!" Branch ordered, and once again, something in his voice prevented the small prisoner from being attacked by the Teutonic peace officer. "You're way too quick to temper, *amigo.*"

"Can you blame me for *that*?" Soehnen demanded bitterly.

"Nope, I can't come out all truth-ical and say I do," the elderly sergeant admitted. "Only there's all them son-of-a-bitching soft shells* up to Austin and beyond to think about, hoping Miz Minnie'll 'scuse me for using such words in her hearing.

* "Soft shell": Derogatory name for a radical "liberal" with "humanitarian" views. *J.T.E.*

They don't reckon's how it's right 'n' proper that us peace officers should go a-whomping no miss-cree-aunt over the head
when all he's done's help rape and half kill a li'l gal imp-er-lite-
like. 'Cording to them, the police in Bolshevik Russia wouldn't
do no such thing."

"He's lying in his teeth about his sidekick, though," the Chicano Ranger claimed, joining his companions. "Way I heard it,
they were still running together when they wide-looped that
Hudson in the parking lot over to Sierra Blanca."

"I didn't reckon's he'd be telling the truth," Branch confessed, favoring Clint with a scowl. "Comes a point, I don't
reckon's how he'd tell you-all yes was you to ask if Monday
comes a day afore Tuesday. But, knowing how close him and
that other varmint stick together, I'll bet all I've got—which
ain't a whole heap, being honest—they've fixed up to ran-diss-
voice here, like they used to say over in France when I was there
with ole Black Jack* and the A.E.F.**

"So all we need do is lay up here and wait for that bastard
Blood to come," Carlos Franco stated rather than suggested,
stroking the barrel of his carbine almost affectionately. "I don't
reckon we'll be lucky enough to take him alive, or unarmed like
this one was, but we'll surely nail his hide to the wall when he
shows."

"You can't do *that*!" Minnie protested, striding forward in an
agitated fashion as she contemplated the detrimental effect such
a proposal could have on her business.

"Ain't *nothing* in the penal code of this-here great 'n' sovereign State of Texas, nor in the Constitution of the whole United
States for that matter, says we can't," Branch contradicted. "Us

---

* General John Joseph "Black Jack" Pershing, (1860–1948) commander-
in-chief of the American Expeditionary Force in Europe during World War
I. *J.T.E.*
** One incident that occurred during Sergeant Jubal Branch's service with
the American Expeditionary Force is described in Case One, "Jubal
Branch's Lucky B.A.R.," *You're a Texas Ranger, Alvin Fog. J.T.E.*

duly sworn peace officers have the legal right to lay in wait for a wanted criminal in *any* place we've got good cause to figure he'll show."

"I hope you-all won't have any objections to me making a telephone call and asking for a second opinion on *that*?" the madam challenged.

"You can call Reece Mervyn, should you-all be so inclinerated, Mizz Minnie," the elderly sergeant assented. "But, for all him being good ole Hogan Turtle's head he-whooper legal shyster, I reckon he'll go along with what I said."

"And what if he doesn't agree with *your* point of view, *Sergeant*?" the madam inquired, despite a feeling that she was approaching a trap.

"Should such *happen,* Miz Minnie," Branch replied, exuding a mildness that—knowing him very well—the madam found most disconcerting, "while you're at it, ask him what-all's the pen-ul-tery for selling in-tox-erating lick-yers against the Prohibitical law's them blasted Yankee pussyfooters* up to Washington, D.C., brought in back to nineteen."

"I don't know what you mean!" Minnie claimed, but without any great conviction and—before she could prevent herself from committing the indiscretion—her gaze swung to the glasses in front of the three cowhands, each of which still held sufficient liquor to establish her guilt.

"Well now, put it *this* way," Branch replied. "I wouldn't want to bet nothing hay-tall that what those young fellers're drinking'll turn out to be sass-par-illy, nor even Limey tea. So, things being's they be 'n' much's we'd miss-like doing meanness to a for-real lady like *you,* Miz Minnie, it's our bounden 'n' legal'-appointed duty to uphold said Prohibitical law. The bomber

---

* "Pussyfooter": Used in this context, a sanctimonious person who had supported the Volstead Act. *J.T.E.*

boys'd* be all riled up should they hear's how we *hadn't* and'd
for certain sure complain to Maj' Benson Tragg. Of course, was
we'n able to say's how we'd had something more important to
take our minds offen what we'd seen—"

"Like laying in wait for that—*gentleman*'s—companion?" the
madam hinted, darting yet another baleful glare at the small
Texan who was the cause of all her misfortunes, as the elderly
peace officer's words trailed to an end.

"Well, yes," Branch agreed, sounding as if the idea had never
occurred to him. "I reckon that'd do it."

"I don't need to call Mr. Mervyn," Minnie surrendered. "But
please try to be inconspicuous while you're waiting and I'd prefer you to try to take him outside. I'd hate to have blood and
bullet holes everywhere."

"Why, sure, ma'am," Branch promised. "Seeing's how we'll
be dealing with a cuss's wolf-smart's that young Comanche
Blood's showed hisself, we'll not be letting ourselves get seen
any too promin-entary. Top of which, him being so all-fired
ornery, we don't exactly aim to let him come to hand-shaking
distance afore we calls on him to yell calf rope."

"Thank you," the madam answered, knowing that the term
calf rope was used by cowhands to indicate surrender.

"I've been thinking some on how we take Blood, Jubal,"
Soehnen remarked. "Like you-all said, he's such a slick son of a
bitch and all, it'd maybe be better if I was to take Clint to the
pokey in El Paso so he's out of you boys' way."

"I dunno about that, Dutchy," Branch objected. "It'd leave
us two short to lay for Blood."

"Two short?" Soehnen repeated. "How come there'll be *two*
short?"

---

* "bomber boys," also known as the "revenuers": Investigators in the Enforcement Branch of the Internal Revenue Service's Alcohol and Tobacco
Tax Division. *J.T.E.*

"You 'n' whoever goes along to ride shotgun for you," the elderly sergeant elaborated.

"Hell, I don't need *anybody* along with me!" the Germanic Ranger stated truculently. "Day I can't handle a short-growed runt like him, with him handcuffed to boot, I'll know it's time for me to turn in my badge."

"I'm not gainsaying you couldn't," Branch declared. "Worrying thing to me, though, 's just how you-all might be figuring to handle him along the way."

"What's that mean?" Soehnen demanded.

"I know just how you-all feel about that li'l German gal they mishandled so bad up to Cowtown," Branch answered, ignoring the fact that everybody else in the reception room was able to overhear what should have been a confidential conversation. "Which I don't blame you none for that, seeing's how I feel just about the same on it. Thing being, though, happen you've got any notions along such lines, Maj' Tragg won't stand for none of that greaser *ley fuega* being done on prisoners took by his company."*

"Who cares what the major won't stand for?" Soehnen challenged.

"I do," Branch replied. "Which seeing's I'm the sergeant—"

"And so am I!" the Germanic Ranger interrupted. "So don't pull rank on *me.*"

"I wouldn't want to do that," Branch protested. "It's you's I'm thinking about—"

*"Gracias,"* Soehnen said sarcastically. As he continued there was a lack of conviction in his voice and manner. "I'll make sure he doesn't have anything to stand for. And, should you leave that short-growed son of a bitch stay here, you'll need at

---

* *"Ley fuega,"* sometimes called the "law of the trail": A colloquial name for a habit attributed to Mexican law enforcement agencies, whereby a prisoner would be ordered to run away and then shot on the pretext that he was trying to escape. *J.T.E.*

least two of us to watch him. Even then he might find some way of warning the half-breed we're waiting."

"There's *that* to it," Branch conceded. Then, with his demeanor warning he would brook no argument, he went on. "Tell you what, Dutchy. You-all take *both* these jaspers in and you can go."

"*Both* of them?" Soehnen said somberly, looking from Clint to the New Yorker and back. "That could prove more'n a mite chancy."

"Not the way I aim to fix things," the elderly sergeant replied reassuringly. "Come on over here, Mr. Torreson."

"Not while that something dog's watching me!" the fugitive refused, looking in alarm at the apparently somnolent and docile bluetick.

"Shuckens, ole Lightning won't fuss none with you-all," Branch asserted, then continued after a pause pregnant with warning. "Not so long's he sees you're coming *toward* me, 'stead of trying to sneak out like last time."

Keeping a wary eye on the dog, although his instincts told him it would not be allowed to attack him unless he provided provocation, the New Yorker walked across the room. A glance over his shoulder informed him that the bluetick was following, but in a manner that implied it was on the verge of collapse. His earlier experiences warned him its appearance was most deceptive.

On reaching the elderly sergeant, while the dog lay down once more, Torreson had both his wrists released. He was not, however, permitted to take his arms from behind his back. Instead, at Branch's orders, Clint was pushed alongside him. With the muzzle of Soehnen's trench gun pressing against the center of his chest, in mute testimony to the caution that the peace officers felt was necessary when dealing with him, the small Texan was liberated just as briefly. Then his right arm was taken across behind his back and handcuffed to the other prisoner's left wrist.

"I don't reckon either of 'em'll be able to move around any too spry, hitched up together that ways," branch drawled with satisfaction at the conclusion of the securing. "And I'll be keeping the keys to the cuffs, Dutchy, just so there'll be no chance of them getting loose accidenticallike 'n' making you-all need to shoot 'em."

"No chance at all, I'd say," the blond Ranger admitted, sounding more bitter than relieved over the precaution. "Here, *you* might's well keep this old cornsheller." After the elderly sergeant had relieved him of the trench gun, which still left him carrying the two Colt Government model automatic pistols on his person, he addressed the prisoners in a voice charged with menace. "All right, you pair, march outside and get aboard our truck. You'd best make good and sure that short-growed son of a bitch don't try anything, Torreson. I've no quarrel with *you*, but I won't let that stop me fixing his wagon any old way I need to, and you're close enough to be in the line of fire."

# 6

# I'D HAVE KILLED
# HIM ANYWAYS

"What the hell?" Hans "Dutchy" Soehnen exclaimed, hearing a pop and the hiss of escaping air from the right front tire of the Pierce-Arrow truck.

Leaving Sergeant Jubal Branch and the other members of the raiding party to start making preparations for the reception of Rapido Clint's companion, Comanche Blood,* the blond Texas Ranger had followed the two prisoners into the cab of the vehicle in which the peace officers had made their undetected arrival at the Premier Chicken Ranch. Once they set out for El Paso, it was soon obvious that he was in no hurry to reach their destina-

---

* Among other things, on their recovery, Sergeant Jubal Branch silenced the objections of Brian Molyneux and his companions to remaining by pointing out that Jackson Speight was guilty of assaulting the black bartender and Terrence Lacey had tried to attack Minnie Lassiter. He had said no charges would be filed against them, provided they cooperated by staying until the ambush was brought to its conclusion. Having no wish for it to become known they had been at the Premier Chicken Ranch, they agreed. *J.T.E.*

tion. Even after turning from the mouth of the canyon on to the road, he had kept the speed down to little more than twenty miles per hour.

Although no conversation had passed between them, Victor Torreson had suspected the leisurely pace was being employed in the hope that the small Texan would say or do something that would allow Soehnen to take punitive action. However, if the summation was correct, it had not achieved its purpose. Held close to the New York fugitive by the far from comfortable way in which their outside arms were shackled together, Clint had sat silently gazing out of the right side window. There had, in Torreson's opinion, been nothing for him to see apart from the fairly open rolling range country on either side. Nor did anything of interest happen for the first mile and a half they traveled.

On the sudden and unexpected deflation of the tire, the truck swerved slightly. However, it was only traveling slowly and the Ranger had no difficulty in keeping it under control. Having brought it to a halt, he leaned forward and gazed past his prisoners in a suspicious fashion. There was no sign of human life on either side of the road, and the nearest cover that would offer concealment for anything larger than a jackrabbit was a clump of bushes on a rim almost half a mile to the right. Being an experienced peace officer, Soehnen scanned the foliage for a few seconds. Then, having satisfied himself there was nothing to fear from that direction, he shoved open the left side door of the cab. In spite of believing the blowout had been accidental, he eased himself from the vehicle in an alert, wary, and watchful manner.

"All right, you two!" the Ranger growled, drawing the Colt Government model automatic pistol from the holster on his gunbelt. "Let's have you both out of there. Come real slow and easy!"

"Now that's what I call a right smart john law, Mr. Torreson," Clint drawled derisively, turning his attention away from the right side of the road. "Hitched together the way we are, just how the hell could one or the other of us stay behind, was we a mind to do it?"

"Watch your lip, you short-growed son of a bitch!" Soehnen barked, gesturing with his pistol. "I said get your asses out here!"

"You-all heard the man, Mr. Torreson," the small Texan stated, reaching across with his free left hand toward the handle of the right side door. "We'd best do what he says, afore he gets so riled he bites himself between the ears."

"Not that way, goddamn it!" Soehnen snapped. "Come out here!"

"This side'll be easi—" Clint began.

"You heard me!" the Ranger shouted, showing that his temper was wearing thin.

"Come on!" Torreson ordered, beginning to move in the required direction. Then, remembering the difficulty they had experienced when boarding through the passenger door, he went on to the man to whom he was secured. "And watch how you follow me. I don't want my wrist cut by these goddamned handcuffs."

"Now don't you-all go getting into a muck-sweat, Mr. Torreson," Clint advised as he moved after the New Yorker. "Seeing's I'm just as likely as you to get cut open, I'll treat you 'most as gentle as I would a newborn lamb." Lowering his voice to a pitch that the other was only just able to hear, he continued urgently. "Keep awake once we're out of here. Should I make a move, be ready to go along with me."

Shuffling slowly across the seat, followed by the small Texan, the fugitive from New York controlled the surprise elicited by the cryptic utterance. Although he did not attempt to ask any questions, realizing that his companion in misfortune must be contemplating some form of escape bid, he was perturbed by the possibility. Nor could he see how the other could hope to bring it about.

He remembered how Clint had been more than holding his

own against the three larger, heavier men in the reception room at the Premier Chicken Ranch; also he recalled the careful way in which the Rangers had treated him even after he was handcuffed. Torreson did not doubt he was a remarkably competent fighting man, but for all that, there did not appear to be anything positive he could do in their present situation. The effectiveness of the elderly sergeant's unconventional way of coupling them together was demonstrated in the extremely cumbersome fashion in which they were being compelled to move. Furthermore, even if the small Texan had been at liberty to make a sudden bound, Soehnen was standing too far away to be reached, and he held a gun.

Despite having a very good reason for wishing to attain his liberty, the New Yorker could not imagine how Clint could overcome the serious handicap under which they were placed. He did not doubt that the Ranger would not hesitate to shoot, should an excuse be presented, and he decided he must prevent the intended "move" if it seemed likely to be one that was doomed to failure. He did not want his own life placed in jeopardy.

In spite of sensing the alarm his words had caused, with Soehnen watching them, the small Texan knew he could not set the other prisoner's mind at ease by making an explanation. Instead, as soon as his feet were on the ground, he reached behind his back with his free hand.

Like the Garnell brothers earlier, when searching Clint, Ranger Carlos Franco had failed to appreciate the potential offered by the round-ended stick as a weapon in his right hip pocket. Nor had there been any reference to its capabilities back at the Chicken Ranch. None of the onlookers had noticed it being put into use during the fight with the three troublemakers. What was more, the two participants who might have warned how effective it could be, having received a practical demonstration, were still unconscious and unable to supply the information. So, where a firearm, knife, or knuckle-duster would have been confiscated, the harmless-looking device was left in his possession.

"Hey there, Dutchy," the small Texan said in a mocking tone, contriving to take the stick from his pocket, the movements being shielded from the Ranger's view by his proximity to Torreson. "Was that li'l ole German gal up to Cowtown any kin to you-all?"

"She wasn't," Soehnen answered. "Or you wouldn't have lived long enough to be asking about it."

"Well now, coming to think of it, I should have known she just *couldn't* be," Clint went on, still employing a derisive manner of speaking. "Happen she had been kin to *you-all*, she'd likely have been too goddamned ugly for ole Comanch' and me t—"

"Shut your goddamned mouth, you son of a bitch!" the Germanic Ranger thundered, starting to move forward, but he did not allow his obvious anger to lead him completely into indiscretion and he kept his automatic pointing in the direction of the two prisoners. "Or I'll do i—"

Guessing what Clint was trying to bring about, and having mixed emotions about it, the thoughts of the New York fugitive on what to do for the best were interrupted before he could reach any decision.

The same means that affected Torreson also brought Soehnen's heated words to an end.

Once again, with nothing to suggest how it happened, there had been a pop and the hissing of liberated air. This time, it was the right rear tire that suffered the blowout.

Startled by the unexpected sounds, the Ranger looked in the general direction from which they had originated. While doing so, Soehnen inadvertently allowed his weapon to waver out of its alignment.

The purely involuntary action proved to be a grave error.

Instantly—either taking advantage of an opportunity presented by chance, or because he had been expecting something of the sort to happen—Clint went into action with the kind of speed that had earned him his sobriquet.

Swiveling his torso to the right with great rapidity, the small Texan slipped his left arm forward between himself and Torreson. His goading tactics had failed to bring Soehnen quite close enough, so he had to move nearer himself. Hoping that the man to whom he was shackled would draw the required conclusion, he began to do so.

Clint's unheralded and hurried advance caused a warning pull to be exerted upon the New Yorker's handcuffed left wrist. Realizing what was happening, he had sufficient presence of mind to save himself from a possible injury by twisting hurriedly in that direction. As he was starting to move, he saw the small Texan's stick-filled fist lashing out. Because of the speed at which he was moving, although he heard the sound of the blow, he did not see it land. However, upon looking over his shoulder, he discovered that it had been at least partially successful.

Despite having lost his Stetson, which must have been knocked from his head when he was hit by the stick, the Germanic Ranger still held the automatic pistol. However, as it was dangling loosely by his side and the muzzle pointed harmlessly toward the ground, it no longer posed any immediate threat. Nor did there appear to be any likelihood of it being brought into use any too quickly. As he stumbled backward on unsteady legs, the Ranger's other hand was clasped to the side of his head and blood ran redly from beneath it. Years of erosion by countless sets of wheels and other use had made the road somewhat lower than the terrain through which it had been carved. When his boots caught against the raised verge as he continued his involuntary retreat, he toppled backward and the pistol slipped from his grasp.

"Come on!" Clint snapped, dropping the stick that had once again proved to be a most effective weapon. He lunged forward without awaiting a reply from the man to whom he was attached.

For the second time, in spite of being taken unawares, Torreson was able to respond swiftly enough to avoid having his arm wrenched and possibly damaged by the handcuffs. However, although the way they were connected caused him to walk backward, he felt no resentment over being put to such an inconvenience. Nor, as he was satisfied that there was no immediate danger of reprisals from their captor, had he any qualms over allowing the small Texan to continue to control the situation. Short in stature though he undoubtedly was, Clint had proved to be remarkably competent up to that point and he still clearly knew what he was doing.

Watching the small Texan scooping up the pistol that Soehnen had dropped, a sensation of mingled elation and relief filled the New York fugitive. Although he still could not understand how the escape had been brought about, beyond feeling certain that the fortuitous blowouts could not have happened purely by chance, he was no longer a prisoner of the Texas Rangers. Even without having any means of transport—being disinclined to try to retrieve his horse from the combined garage and stable of the Premier Chicken Ranch and doubting whether, even if the blowouts could be repaired, the truck would serve his purpose—he would have no special difficulty in reaching and crossing the Rio Grande. Once having attained the safety of Mexican soil, he would continue walking into Juarez and complete the remainder of his journey by taxi.

"Sorry I didn't have the chance to tell you what I was figuring on doing, friend," Clint remarked, straightening up and looking over his shoulder at Torreson as he hefted the big Colt with an air of satisfaction. "I didn't hurt you-all when I jumped this son of a bitch, did I?"

"No, I saw what was coming and moved with you," the New Yorker replied, noticing that the slightly derisive "Mr. Torreson" was no longer employed by his rescuer. "Thanks for getting us out of it."

"We're not all the way out of it yet," Clint warned, tucking the automatic pistol into his waistband.

"Hell, no!" Torreson admitted. The slight tug on the hand-cuffs caused by the small Texan's movements brought a memory of what had happened shortly before they boarded the truck at the brothel. "That mother-something old bastard with the mutt kept the keys, so how are we going to get out of these 'cuffs?"

"Reckon ole Comanch' will have to do it for us," Clint replied, turning slowly so he could look over the hood of the truck toward the right side of the trail.

"Who?" Torreson asked, then stared in the same direction. "So *that's* how come the blowouts happened!"

"I don't reckon either of us has lived right enough for Divine Providence to have decided we needed a helping hand," Clint commented dryly. "Though they do say the Devil looks after his own, which there's some might reckon's just what's happened."

"Who is he?" the New Yorker asked, still staring at the figure which was now approaching them from the bushes just below the rim.

"My *bueno amigo,*" the small Texan answered. "Known to the john laws and other good friends's Comanche Blood."

"The one they're laying for at the Chicken Ranch?" Torreson guessed.

"The self-same, original, and only one," Clint confirmed. "I figured it must be him when the first tire blew out. Only there wasn't enough cover for him on the left side, so's he could nail that son-of-a-bitching squarehead once we'd stopped and got out. Which left it to me to take him out. Come along with me while I get his other gun."

While complying with the suggestion, the fugitive from New York studied the person whose intervention had paved the way for his and Clint's escape from custody.

Around six foot in height, slender in build, the man strolling down the slope appeared to be in his late twenties. A white Texas-style straw hat, with an eagle feather rising from its In-

dian bead band, was perched on the back of his head and added
to his height. It also showed he had rusty-red hair of moderate
length and a handsome, darkly tanned face. Clad in the attire of
a working cowhand, each item of which had seen considerable
hard use, he had on a pair of Comanche-made moccasins instead of the more usual high-heeled and sharp-toed riding boots.
He moved with a long, effortless striding gait indicative of hard
and powerful muscles in his lean frame. A hunting knife with an
ivory hilt hung in a sheath on the left side of his waist belt.
Across the crook of his right arm rested a magnificent imported
Holland & Holland .375 magnum sporting rifle, to which was
attached the latest type of telescopic sight and a silencer of a
kind Torreson had never seen before.

"Howdy, you-all," the newcomer greeted on reaching the
road. "I told you to keep away from that fancy cathouse,
Rapido."

"You told me," the small Texan conceded, having collected
the second automatic from the motionless and, judging from the
lack of resistance, unconscious Soehnen. "I'll *maybe* listen to
you next time."

"I wouldn't want to take bets on it," the dark young man
declared.

"And you'd be wise not to," Clint confessed. "How's about
you-all getting these goddamned 'cuffs off for us, Comanch'?
Those sneaky sons of bitches kept the keys with them when they
sent us off to the jail-house."

"I'll do my damnedest, *amigo*," Comanche Blood promised
and went on with a grin, "Don't reckon you'll let me *shoot* 'em
off? I saw it done in a movie one time."

"You *don't* reckon all too goddamned right, you *loco* Indian!"
the small Texan affirmed, also grinning. "No matter what they
did in that son-of-a-bitching movie, you come up with a safer
way."

"Could maybe just set on our butts here until you-all both
starved down a mite 'n' can slip your hands free," the newcomer

suggested, glancing at the truck. "Only I can't see you-all wanting to do that neither. So there's only but one thing for it. Let's see what-all's in the toolbox."

"I thought you'd never get around to asking," Clint drawled as he and the fugitive from New York followed the young man toward the vehicle. "Hey, though, you-all don't know each other. Like I told you just now, Mr. Torreson, this here's my *bueno amigo,* Comanche Blood. Comanch', say Howdy, you-all right polite to Mr. Victor Torreson."

"Whee-dogie!" the lean Texan exclaimed, looking at the New Yorker with more interest than he had displayed up to that moment. "Not *the* Mr. Victor Torreson, late of li'l ole New York City? Him that's hiring guns down to Juarez?"

"The very same," Clint confirmed.

"Well, I'll swan!" Blood declared. "Ole *Ka-Dih*'s* sure looking favorable on this quarter *Pehnane* boy this day!"

"How did you know I'm hiring guns?" demanded the Mexican-dressed fugitive, looking from one to the other Texan.

"Didn't figure's how you was trying so all-fired hard to keep it a secret," Blood answered. "We heard tell about it all the way up to good ole Tobias Crumley's tavern, out Grande Prairie way and, being in need of gainful employment, as Rapido called it, concluded to drift on down 'n' see happen you could use us."

"You'll have to take that up with my boss," Torreson warned, knowing the establishment to which Blood had referred was a regular hangout for criminals of all kinds. "But he *always* goes along with what I say."

Having opened the toolbox while delivering the explanation, Blood was looking inside. A grunt of satisfaction broke from him as he produced a hammer and a cold chisel. As he lowered the vehicle's tailgate, he told the prisoners to place their manacled wrists on the metal frame of the bed. After climbing aboard by the time this was accomplished, he knelt down. Then, plac-

---

* *Ka-Dih:* the Great Spirit, supreme deity of the Comanche nation. *J.T.E.*

ing the tip of the chisel carefully on to the center of the hand-
cuff's swivel link, he severed it with blows from the hammer.

"I can't do anything more for you right now. You'll have to
wait until we can lay hands on a hacksaw afore we get the rest
off," Blood apologized, jumping from the back of the truck.
"Come on. I've got some hosses hid out over the rim and they'll
tote us to your place easy 'n' comfortable, Mr. Torreson."

*"Some?"* Clint queried.

"Were four of them when I got there and damned if I could
decide which was the best two, so I fetched them all along and
their saddles," the Texan explained. A low groan sounded from
the left side of the road. Instead of supplying further information about the acquisition of the horses, Blood looked around
and went on, "Looks like you-all didn't hit that son-of-a-bitching john law hard enough, Rapido."

"Looks that way," the small Texan admitted, also glancing
and stepping away from the other two. "This just *isn't* his day,
though."

Completing the comment in such a mild-seeming tone it gave
no indication of his intentions, Clint swung toward the cause of
the disturbance. He had tucked the two Colt automatic pistols
into his waistband. After liberating one with his left hand, he
brought it to shoulder height after the fashion of a target
shooter. Taking aim at where the Ranger was starting to sit up,
he squeezed the trigger twice as quickly as the mechanism could
operate and, ejecting the spent case, replenished the chamber
with the uppermost round in the magazine.

Watching, Torreson saw two holes appear in the left breast of
Soehnen's calfskin vest. Then he was slammed backward once
more.

"You killed him!" The New Yorker grunted, impressed by the
speed with which the deed had been carried out.

"Seemed like a good thing to do," the small Texan replied.
"We couldn't've just rode off and left him here to spread that

we've got away. But I'd have killed him anyways. Nobody knocks down Rapido Clint and lives. Let's get going, shall we?"

Accompanying the two Texans up the right slope, which prevented him from making a closer examination of the Ranger who had been shot, Torreson was pretty well satisfied with the way things had turned out. Not only had he escaped from the clutches of the law, which would almost certainly have seen him ending his days in the electric chair at Sing Sing,* but he had also acquired two very competent fighting men for his employer's entourage. There was only one thing left undone. Circumstances over which he had no control prevented him from arranging all the details of the assignment that had inadvertently led to his being captured. He did not doubt that this could be dealt with over the telephone after he was safely outside the United States.

---

* "Sing Sing": State prison near Ossining, New York. *J.T.E.*

# 7

# I WANT
# RAPIDO CLINT, DEAD

"Know something, Miz Minnie?" Sergeant Jubal Branch inquired, sitting at ease in the comfortable chair at the desk of the madam, which about half an hour earlier had been occupied by Victor Torreson. He was studying a glass of far better bourbon than was offered to his predecessor. "Being's rank's I am surely does have its privet-icals."

"Jubal Branch," Minnie Lassiter replied with a smile from her chair at the other side of the desk, waving a bejeweled left hand to where the big bluetick coonhound was sprawling, apparently asleep, by the interior door of her private office. "The way you mangle English is about as near the truth as the way that fool Lightning dog is behaving."

"Why, I surely don't know what you mean, Miz Minnie," the elderly peace officer declared in tones of puzzlement. "I'm just a half-smart, un-edic-itatured ole country boy who don't know no better."

"If you're only half-smart," the madam asserted, "I'd hate to run up against somebody who's all-smart."*

While the thorough preparations for the reception of Comanche Blood had been completed to Branch's exacting satisfaction, he was unaware that events elsewhere had rendered them a waste of time. He had accepted Minnie's invitation to join her in the office ostensibly for a cup of coffee. Despite the means by which he had obtained her cooperation in the matter of using her premises as the site for the intended ambush, he had not seen fit to either invoke the "Prohibitical" law or refer to the "bomber boys" when the beverage she produced proved to be a bottle of Wild Turkey bourbon. Instead, he had agreed that an excessive consumption of coffee could possibly be injurious to health, and had accepted a glass filled with the liquor.

At first, neither hostess nor guest had done anything more than sip at their drinks with the air of connoisseurs. However, although the pose was true in so far as Branch had a well-developed taste for good liquor, he had been wondering why the invitation had been given. Minnie and he had known each other for a number of years and had a mutual liking and respect. For all that, neither had ever forgotten that—to all intents and purposes—they were on opposite sides of the law. As she had always been scrupulously honest, according to her lights, this had never brought them into open conflict. On the other hand, while their divergent ways of life had never prevented her from offering hospitality whenever their paths had crossed, he guessed there was something more that had impelled her to do so on this occasion. Suspecting what it could be, he was looking forward

---

* Alvin Dustine "Cap" Fog claims that the mispronunciation of words by Sergeant Jubal Branch was merely a pose intended to make miscreants assume he was far less intelligent than was the case. We are inclined to believe this. Certainly all of his reports that Cap allowed us to examine were written in a far more legible hand than our own. Furthermore, the spelling and grammar were impeccable. *J.T.E.*

to the verbal fencing with which he meant to circumvent her desire for information.

The comment about rank having its privileges had been intended to open the conversation. It allowed the elderly sergeant to satisfy his curiosity, while preventing the madam from discovering whether her suspicions were correct.

"Land's sakes a-mercy, Miz Minnie!" Branch protested. "You'll be making me take to blushing, should you-all keep on talking that way."

"I'll have to try to spare you *that,*" the madam answered blandly, then continued in the tone of one who was making no more than innocently casual and time-passing conversation. "But I didn't know you'd started working in this area."

"Well, you-all know how it is with us Rangers," Branch replied in a similar fashion, feeling even more sure his suppositions over the reason for the invitation were correct. "Man no sooner gets hisself settled than those high mucky-mucks up to Austin figure it's time to move him around."

"They seem to have been doing rather a lot of moving around, going by what I saw in the reception room," Minnie commented. "The last I heard, Dutchy Soehnen was with Company A at Fort Worth."

"What he said's he came down this way hunting Rapido Clint and Comanche Blood," the elderly sergeant explained. "Called on us to lend him a hand, them being so slick, tricky, and ornery."

"Is that why Benny Goldberg and Colin Breda came down here?" the madam inquired, referring to two other members of the posse. "They usually work with Company C over in the Panhandle country, don't they?"

"They've worked there on occasion-ical," Branch conceded, then went on with the air of one who was proving a point. "But *everybody* know's how good ole Carlos Franco's allus been riding the border country down along the river here."

"I'm not gainsaying *that,*" Minnie replied. "Any more than

you could say David Swift-Eagle *hasn't* been keeping watch on the Oklahoma line for the past five years at least. And there's dear Frenchie Giradot. Whatever will the girls down in Galveston do now he isn't around town any more?"

"Likely the same's they've been having to since he up and got hisself all 'matrimon-ialized' last fall," Branch answered, sounding as if the peace officer in question had contracted some particularly unpleasant disease instead of having taken a wife. "Without him. Anyways, young fellers these days don't take over kind to staying for too long in the same neck of the woods."

"So it seems," the madam conceded and, for the first time, there was just a trace of irony in her voice. "I'll say one thing, though. Benson Tragg is either a very lucky man, or he must have powerful friends in high places, to have so many extremely experienced and capable officers transferred to his company at the same time."

"There's some folks's reckons's how the major was born under a right fortune-atical star," the elderly sergeant admitted as unemotionally as ever. Tragg—a cousin of the sheriff of El Paso County—was the commanding officer of his company. "Which, seeing's how he's had *me* serving along of him for the past four years, there's others allow such can't be so."

"I wouldn't want to comment one way or the other on *that.*" Minnie smiled, then became more serious. "How long have Rapido Clint and Comanche Blood been on the run?"

"Ever since they—"

A knock on the interior door prevented the sergeant from completing his explanation. Although he and the madam both looked in that direction, the big bluetick never so much as stirred.

"Some watchdog *he* makes!" Minnie sniffed in mock disdain, deducing from the lack of reaction shown by the apparently somnolent animal that one of Branch's companions was requesting admittance. Raising her voice, she called, "Come in, please!"

"Sorry to interrupt you at coffee, Miz Minnie," apologized Alexandre "Frenchie" Giradot, entering with his boater in his hand and ignoring the bottle of Wild Turkey on the desk. Turning his gaze to the other peace officer, he went on. "No sign of Blood so far, Jubal. Has Dutchy called in yet?"

"Not yet," Branch replied. He had instructed Hans "Dutchy" Soehnen to report immediately on reaching the jail in El Paso. Looking as near to being worried as his features ever did, he addressed the woman. "Mind if I use your telephone, Miz Minnie?"

"Feel free," the madam replied without hesitation. Having found the conversation interesting and intriguing, although it had done nothing to answer the speculations that had prompted her invitation, she hoped to be able to continue talking after the call had been made. "Can I offer you a—cup of coffee—Frenchie?"

"Not while I'm on duty, Miz Minnie," the Gallic-looking Ranger answered, as the other peace officer was lifting the earpiece from the hooks of the telephone's candlestick pedestal mount.

"He hasn't got there yet!" Branch announced, hanging up after a brief conversation with the deputy sheriff in charge of the jail at El Paso. He had ended the call by a request that Soehnen should call the Premier Chicken Ranch as soon as he arrived with his prisoners.

"He should have by now!" Giradot stated, showing somewhat more concern than was discernible on the older lawman's leathery visage.

"That's for sure!" Branch seconded, rising with a gesture of impatience. "God damn it all, Frenchie. If he's took them off someplace so's he can work Clint over, much's that short-growed son of a bitch deserves it, Major Tragg'll have his badge so fast he'll think the hawgs've jumped him."

"Jubal!" Ranger Carlos Franco said, coming into the office at a waddling run and without the formality of requesting permission to enter. "Could be something's up. The major's headed along the canyon like his butt's on fire."

"The hell you say!" Branch barked. After picking up and draining the glass, he nodded at his hostess and went on. "Thanks for the . . . coffee . . . Miz Minnie!"

The sergeant then set down the glass and strode swiftly toward the door. He was followed into the reception room by the other two Rangers and the bluetick, who came to its feet with a complete change of manner from its former somnolence and went after them.

"Darn the luck!" Minnie breathed, picking up the bottle and glasses to place them in the drawer of the desk from which they had been produced. After closing the drawer, she rose and started to walk across the office, continuing equally quietly, "Not that I was getting anywhere with you, you cagey old devil, but it was fun trying and there was *just* a chance I'd learn *why* Benson Tragg has had all *those* men transferred to his company."

On entering the reception room, the madam's thoughts were diverted from why—in spite of her extensive connections with the criminal element, as a result of being high in the hierarchy of Hogan Turtle's organization, she had never heard of two such obviously competent lawbreakers as Rapido Clint and Comanche Blood. From the sounds that came to her ears, the car that was arriving was being driven at some speed until it was in front of the house, instead of having halted in the parking lot. Even before its engine stopped, hurried footsteps were crossing the porch. Although the Garnell brothers were in their usual positions outside, having been sent back on duty by Branch to make everything look normal in case Blood should put in the anticipated appearance, they did not stop to search the newcomer.

Striding rapidly across the threshold of the reception room, Benson Tragg looked more like a prosperous rancher than a major in the Texas Rangers, except for the grim expression on his tanned face. A good six feet tall, with a build as lean and wiry as that of Jubal Branch, he conveyed the impression of being a man who followed a strenuous and active occupation. Brown haired, going gray at the temples, in his late forties, he wore a lightweight bronze straw hat with a Luskey roll crease— indicating it had been purchased at the Lone Star State's premier western wear store—a brown suit, white shirt, red-, white-, and blue-striped necktie, and Justin boots. Although the jacket was of excellent cut, the tailor had not been able to make it hang so that it completely hid the bulge made by the walnut-handled, short-barreled Colt Storekeeper model Peacemaker revolver holstered, butt forward, on the left side of his waist belt.

"Just why the hell did you let Dutchy Soehnen go off on his own, *Sergeant* Branch?" the newcomer demanded angrily, his accent that of a Texan who had received a good education, as the elderly peace officer advanced with some haste to meet him.

"We took Clint without no trouble," Branch replied, sounding a trifle defensive. "So Dutchy insisted on hauling him straight over to the jailhouse while the rest of us laid up here to wait for Blood."

"*Insisted?*" Tragg repeated. "And *you* let him do it?"

"He just wouldn't have it no other way at all," Branch asserted as Minnie came up behind him. "Which, him being a *sergeant* same's me, I couldn't haul off and order him not to. What's up, Maj', have you-all come across him?"

"I've come across him, for sure!" Tragg confirmed in a bitter tone. "And so had Comanche Blood—a mite earlier!"

"The hell you-all say!" the elderly sergeant exclaimed. "Do you mean that half-breed son of a bitch's *wounded* Dutchy?"

"*Wounded?*" the Major repeated, spitting the word out as if hating the taste of it. For a moment his gaze flickered to the madam. Then, looking back to his obviously alarmed subordinate, he continued just as bitingly. "Well now, seeing that I found Dutchy with *two* goddamned bullet holes in his chest, I reckon you could just about say *somebody* wounded him!"

"How the hell did it happen?" Branch demanded as the rest

of the Rangers gathered around and the other occupants of the reception room displayed an equal interest in what was being said.

"I wouldn't know for sure, not having been there when it happened!" Tragg replied, oozing heavy sarcasm and anger. "But it looks as if Blood made him stop the truck by shooting out the tires with that fancy sporting rifle they wide-looped up to Big D.* Then they got him outside and, unless I'm mistaken, he was shot with his own guns. They're both gone, anyways."

"That'd be Clint's done it," Branch assessed correctly. "Blood'd've used his knife, up so close. How'd they get away?"

"On horseback, according to the sign," Tragg answered. "But there were three sets of foot tracks. Who did they have with them?"

"That Torreson *hombre*'s the New York Police Department want sending back so bad," Branch confessed, and the fact that he did not mispronounce the word department indicated he was deeply perturbed and realized the news would be accorded an unfavorable response by his superior.

*"Torreson?"* The major half gasped and half snarled, confirming the sergeant's suppositions with regard to his reaction. "God damn me to hell, if the governor doesn't beat *Him* to it. *This* is getting *better* by the son-of-a-bitching *minute*—sorry, Miz Minnie, but—" He paused after the apology and made a gesture of resignation bordering on fury, then continued in a no less heated fashion. "So you had *Victor Torreson* in your dainty little hands, *Sergeant* Branch. But you had to let him get *away,* did you?"

"Not *me,* Maj'!" the aged peace officer protested with the kind of righteous indignation that arose out of a guilty conscience and the feeling that he had been found sadly wanting in

---

* "Big D": Colloquial name for the city of Dallas, seat of Dallas County, Texas. *J.T.E.*

carrying out his duty. *"Dutchy Soehnen* was taking 'em in, not me!"

*"You* were in command here!" Tragg pointed out.

*"You* should've been here to tell Dutchy *that!"* Branch countered, half defiant and half resentful. "He's the same rank's me and was set deep 'n' solid to take Clint in, 'stead of waiting here until Blood come. So I reckoned it'd be . . . *safer* . . . was I to send Torreson along of 'em."

"You sent *one* man with *two* goddamned dangerous prisoners?" Tragg asked, his bearing redolent of disbelief.

"Way I hitched 'em together, with their arms behind their backs 'n' Clint's right coupled to Torreson's left," Branch explained in sullen exculpation, "they *couldn't've* jumped him and given him the excuse to—well— You know how Dutchy felt about that li'l German gal's Clint and—"

"I know what you mean!" Tragg interrupted testily, and the onlookers who did not belong to the Texas Rangers assumed he had no desire to let that organization's possibly dirty linen be exposed to public view. "Anyways, I want you bunch to take out after them straightaway. I want Rapido Clint, dead preferably, after the way he gunned Dutchy down, but I'd sooner you fetched in the other two alive if you can."

"Which won't be easy done with Comanch' Blood," Branch warned. "You any idea which way they'll be headed?"

"They were going north from where they mounted the horses, way the sign read," Tragg replied. "But I'd say that Torreson, for one, will swing back so's he can get into Mexico and be clear of the law in the U.S. of A."

"Word has it, his boss is hiring guns," Ranger Colin Breda remarked. Tall, lean, blondish, and craggily good-looking, he was dressed like a working cowhand. He had a Winchester trench gun in his right hand and a Colt Cavalry model Peacemaker hanging holstered from his gunbelt. Despite being a second-generation Texan,* his voice retained a suggestion of "roots" in the Highlands of Scotland. "So Clint and Blood'll likely go along with him. We could maybe head them off at the border."

"Or go over it after the bastards!" suggested Ranger Benjamin "Benny" Goldberg, who looked more like a chubby and jovial storekeeper than the tough and competent peace officer he had proven himself to be.

"Like hell you will!" Tragg declared firmly. "That's *out,* with a capital O U T. No matter how badly we want to nail that son-of-a-bitch Rapido Clint's hide to the wall, there'll be no invading Mexico to do it. See if you can get to the border ahead of them, or find out where they crossed happen you're too late, Ju —Sergeant."

"Yo!" Branch answered, giving the traditional response of the United States cavalry. "How many hosses've you-all got out back's we can borrow 'n' use, Miz Minnie?"

"Four—no, five if you count the General," the madam replied, making the amendment as she remembered that Torreson had arrived on horseback and that the animal was still in the combined garage and stable. "Help yourselves, gentlemen. *You* can use the General if you've a mind, Sergeant Branch."

"Why, thank you 'most to death, ma'am!" the elderly peace officer replied, his gratitude genuine as he knew the animal in question to be the woman's highly prized Tennessee walking horse. "I'll take care of him like he was ole Lightning there."

"You'll find he's somewhat more lively," Minnie warned, glancing to where the bluetick had resumed its lethargic sprawling on the floor.

"He'd *have* to be!" Tragg grunted. "Get going, you bunch. Benny, I want you to come back to El Paso with me. I sent

---

* As is recorded in *.44 Caliber Man* and *A Horse Called Mogollon,* Tam, Ranger Colin Breda's paternal grandfather, had preceded him as a peace officer in Texas. *J.T.E.*

Dutchy in with Paddy Bratton in the other car and I want one or the other of you by his bed at the hospital when—or *if*— he regains consciousness."

Watching the peace officers setting off, the madam frowned. Something struck her as being wrong, but she could not decide exactly what it might be. Her interest in Rapido Clint and Comanche Blood had increased as a result of what she had overheard. Despite their obvious competence, she realized there was a good reason why they had not previously come to her attention. It was possible that they had only recently embarked upon a career of serious crime. In which case, their fame—or notoriety—would not yet have spread extensively. However, although the shooting of Soehnen would make it highly unsafe for them to return to Texas, Hogan Turtle could always find work elsewhere for a pair of their ruthless capability.

Like the peace officers, Minnie felt sure that the two young Texans would accompany Torreson to Albert Brickhouse's *hacienda* near Juarez. In which case, she had a reason for going there. It would allow her to examine them at close quarters and find out what could be learned about them.

# 8
# GUN THE GREASER
# BASTARDS DOWN

*"Madre de Dios, mi amigo!"* Albert Brickhouse enthused jovially, slapping a massive—if flabby—well-jeweled right hand against his more than amply fleshed left thigh, at the conclusion of the explanation that he had requested from Comanche Blood. "That's as smart a piece of work as I've ever heard!"

"Shucks," the Texan replied, shrugging his shoulders and indicating the weapon lying across his lap. "It wasn't so all-fired hard to stop the truck. That son-of-a-bitching German john law was driving so slow I could've been twice's far off and still bust the tire with this ole rifle. It surely is one hell of a straight-shooting gun. Only with me not knowing how fast he'd be coming, I had to lie up on the right—there being no place close enough on the left—so Rapido had to take him out."

Having mounted three of the excellent horses that Blood had acquired, while he led the fourth, Rapido Clint and Victor Torreson had accompanied him to safety. At his instigation, they had started by riding north for a short distance. Then, before turning to the south, they had swung east until they were certain they would be able to cross the road beyond the range of visibility from the entrance to the Premier Chicken Ranch's canyon. They had not seen anybody while on their way to the Rio Grande, arriving there at about the same time that the Texas Rangers were collecting mounts to start hunting for them. Nor had they experienced any particular difficulty in crossing to the Mexican shore. From there, the remainder of their journey had been equally uneventful.

The *hacienda* in which Brickhouse and Torreson had established themselves after fleeing from the law enforcement agencies of the United States was situated in the broken, hilly country about five miles to the southeast of Juarez. Despite the comparative proximity of the city, it had clearly been constructed with the needs of maintaining security against hostile intrusion in mind. Not only were the buildings very sturdily built, they were surrounded by a high and solid wall that had a parapet offering concealment and protection for riflemen, should the need arise.

Apart from attempting the far from easy task of climbing the walls, admittance to the property was through one of the two massive, brass-studded wooden gates. Unless visitors were permitted to enter, these were kept closed and locked, under the watchful attendance of armed guards. In addition, each was covered by a belt-fed .30 caliber Browning 1917 model machine gun mounted in upstairs windows of the main building.

Not including himself and Brickhouse, the New York fugitive had told the Texans as they were crossing the patio from the northern gate to the stables behind the main building, there were a dozen white men on the premises. While this would be insufficient to defend the walls against a determined attack by a large force, they had rifles, trench guns, and a couple of BARs*

---

* BAR: Abbreviation for the Browning automatic rifle. Invented by the remarkably prolific designer of firearms, John Moses Browning (1855–1926)—who makes a guest appearance in *Calamity Spells Trouble*—it was

to augment the machine guns and were adequate protection against any lesser threat. In fact, he had explained, only a desire to prevent trouble with a local *bandido* by a show of greater force was making them hire extra men.

With the horses cared for, the New Yorker had escorted the Texans to the big, spacious, and excellently furnished main building. Stating they preferred to wait until they had met their future companions before starting to act trustful, Clint and Blood had carried their bulky bedrolls with them. Nor had the taller Texan been any more inclined to leave behind his magnificent Holland & Holland .375 Magnum sporting rifle. Having left them in the entrance hall for a short while, Torreson had returned and escorted them into the luxurious library to be introduced to his employer.

Big, corpulent to the point of being grossly flabby, Brickhouse affected the attire of a Mexican *grandee* from an earlier decade, a fashion to which his bulging figure was far from suited. Topped by a thinning thatch of silvery-gray hair, his clean-shaven face would have been guileless if it had not been for his eyes. Appearing smaller than they actually were by surrounding rolls of fat, they were dark and bore a wary, speculative glint that could only have come since his vast and illicit dealings on the stock market had caused him to flee from New York. Certainly it seemed unlikely that they had had such an expression, to give warning of his true character, when he was tricking people and acquiring an estimated million and a half dollars by unscrupulous speculation and blatantly crooked deals. Everything else about his features and demeanor was such as to instill a feeling of confidence. He would have struck most of those with whom he came into contact as a person who could be trusted implicitly—and many people had trusted him, to their cost.

---

intended as a lightweight, portable machine gun for use by infantry. Further details of this weapon can be found in *You're a Texas Ranger, Alvin Fog. J.T.E.*

Clint and Blood were less inclined to trustfulness than the crooked financier's many dupes, but they had still been impressed by his sagacity. They had also been willing to admit that he possessed a knack for making people feel at home in his company. Shaking hands as they were introduced by Torreson, he had employed a surprisingly firm grip, which they concluded must have served him well in the past when dealing with intended victims. After asking them to be seated, he had offered them drinks and smokes. Having supplied them with generous measures of Southern Comfort bourbon and good Havana cigars, he had commented that "Mr. Torreson" was giving them credit for having been rescued from the custody of the Texas Rangers and he had requested further details.

It had soon become apparent that Brickhouse possessed too suspicious a nature to take the two young Texans at face value. He had wanted to know why the Rangers were hunting them, but he put the question so tactfully that neither had taken offense.

Acting as spokesman, Clint had explained that they were wanted for armed robberies they had committed and for molesting a girl in Fort Worth. Seeing no sign of condemnation over the latter, he had confessed that they had been intending to commit another crime to improve their finances before crossing the Rio Grande and visiting the *hacienda* to seek employment. While Blood had been looking for horses upon which to make the journey, the small Texan had visited the Premier Chicken Ranch to study it as a potential target.

"But that's *Minnie Lassiter's* place!" Brickhouse had commented.

"Why, sure," Clint had replied. "We'd heard tell the prices for the girls come high—"

"And it is also owned by Hogan Turtle," the financier interrupted.

"Which's why we figured it'd be worth jumping," the small Texan had asserted. "With *him* owning it, they'd be so sure nobody would dare try to heist them that we'd've have taken them unawares."

"You'd also have had Hogan Turtle's enforcers after you," Brickhouse had pointed out.

"We'd thought on *that,*" Clint had confessed. "But we reckoned, between us, Comanch' and me could have discouraged them."

"After the first 'n's to get sent didn't make it back," Blood had supplemented, "likely the rest would've took the notion it was a mite too dangerous to chance."

"Only, as things turned out, it likely won't come to that," Clint had continued. "Three liquored-up sons of bitches jumped me on the way in. By the time I'd handed them their needings, those goddamned Rangers were inside and throwing down on me."

"*You* beat *three* men?" Brickhouse had said, running his gaze over the small Texan's unimposing figure. Then he went on hurriedly and in a placatory tone. "I'm sorry for appearing to doubt your word, but—"

"Why, sure," Clint had replied, showing no animosity. "I look a mite on the short-grown size to be able to do it. Which's why I could. They were overconfident and didn't know I've learned some pretty fancy and sneaky ways of taking care of myself in a bare-handed fight."

"They was luckier than they'll ever know, for all of that," Blood had injected. "We'd heard tell's how Minnie Lassiter had everybody's went in searched and their weapons took from 'em, so Rapido left his gun with me. Had he been toting it, there'd've been at least three down and made wolf bait* even afore he'd've started in on them son-of-a-bitching john laws."

---

* "Make wolf bait": "To kill." Derived from the practice in the Old West for dealing with carnivores that preyed on stock. An animal would be killed and, having been injected with poison, the carcass was left on the range where it would be found and eaten by the predators. *J.T.E.*

"As it was," Clint had concluded, "with six scatterguns and carbines all pointing at my favorite navel, they had me colder'n an Eskimo's tool. Next thing I knew, they'd picked up Mr. Torreson there and were sending us to the pokey in El Paso. Only ole Comanch' took cards and let us get away before they had us behind bars."

Having been told of the small Texan's adventures, the financier had inquired how his companion had come to be in such a fortuitous position to effect the rescue. Blood had explained how, having stolen the horses they would need, he was waiting in concealment at the opposite side of the road to the entrance of the canyon. Although he had seen the raid on the Premier Chicken Ranch taking place, he had known there was no way he could intervene at that moment. When the prisoners were brought out and made to board the cab of the Pierce-Arrow truck, the way in which they were fastened together had led him to assume correctly what was intended for them, and he had decided to make a rescue attempt.

The discovery that only one Ranger would be accompanying Clint and Torreson had made Blood confident he would be able to set them free with little difficulty or danger, to them. It had been his intention to bring the truck to a halt by puncturing a tire with a bullet from his silenced rifle, then kill the peace officer either in the cab or while an examination of the damage was being made. Unfortunately, he had not been able to find a suitable position on the left side of the road from which to implement the scheme. This had meant he was compelled to make his move from the right, relying on his partner to deduce what was happening and deal with the Ranger when he created a diversion by causing another blowout.

"So what'll we be up against, Mr. Brickhouse?" Clint inquired bluntly, after the financier had praised the dark young man for his foresight and ability.

"Shouldn't think that would worry two tough *hombres* like you," Torreson commented.

"There's a long ways difference between being tough and being stupid," the small Texan answered coldly, looking at the New York fugitive. Then, returning his gaze to Brickhouse, his voice took on a more respectful tone as he went on. "We're neither of us *loco* enough to go into something we wouldn't have a snowball in hell's chance of coming out from alive. Which I don't reckon *you'll* be wanting from us, anyways. But, once we get to know what we'll be up against, it'll let us figure out how much we'll want paying should we take on. I reckon *you-all* can understand *that,* sir?"

"I can," the financier admitted, clearly pleased by the respectful way Rapido was speaking to him. "Hopefully you won't be up against *anything.*"

"Then how come you had word passed that you're hiring?" Clint wanted to know.

"I'm hoping that having some extra men around will allow me to avoid trouble," Brickhouse explained, confirming what the Texans had been told earlier by Torreson. "It's this way, you see. The day after I moved into *Hacienda Naranja,* I had a visit from Cristóbal Guevara and several of his men. He informed me that he was the leader of all the *bandidos* in the area, and it was traditional for the owner of the *hacienda* to pay tribute to him. The price he demanded was reasonable, so I agreed."

"Only it didn't stay reasonable?" Clint guessed.

"It has been increased at ever more regular intervals," Brickhouse confirmed bitterly. "In fact, the price is becoming intolerable."

"You should have figured on *that* from the start," the small Texan declared. "When a game like that is pulled on you and you take it, the feller doing it concludes he's got you buffaloed and can keep shoving up the ante. Best thing you could have done, set up like you are, would've been to say you wouldn't pay a thin dime right from the start."

"That would have led to trouble," the financier pointed out.

"It's either that or keep on paying until you've nothing left to pay with," Clint warned. "When *bandidos* start pulling a game like they are, there's only one way to stop them. Gun the greaser bastards down!"

"If it were only *that* simple!" Brickhouse sighed regretfully. "You see, while I have been allowed to become a Mexican citizen and am on good terms with various government and local authorities, that doesn't apply to them all. There is considerable pressure on Mexico City from the United States to have me extradited, and I have no desire to present the *Guardia Rurales* — with whom I'm *not* on good terms—an excuse to have my naturalization revoked."

"So what do you aim to do?" Clint asked.

"I'm throwing a *fiesta* this weekend and have invited Guevara and his lieutenants as guests of honor," Brickhouse replied, then darted a malevolent gaze at Torreson. "In fact, I hoped to put on a special kind of entertainment that I felt sure would please them, but it seems this won't be possible!"

"God damn it!" the fugitive from New York objected in a resentful voice. "The Rangers were after *Clint,* not *me!*"

"Just what does *that* mean, *hombre?*" the small Texan demanded, coming to his feet, his whole bearing redolent of challenge and menace.

"It wasn't *me* that they were after!" Torreson elaborated, somewhat unnerved by the way in which the strength of Rapido Clint's personality had caused him, suddenly, to take on the size and bulk of a *very* big man. "I'd have gotten clear away if that old bastard with the mutt hadn't happened to come around the corner and stopped me."

*"Happened to?"* Clint repeated and threw a pointed look at Blood. "Did you-all hear *that,* Comanch'?"

"I *heard,* but I'll be somethinged afore I'll believe I *did!*" the dark Texan answered, studying the New York criminal with mingled disbelief and contempt. *"Hombre,* that 'ole bastard with the mutt' as you-all call him is about the smartest god-damned peace officer from here to there 'n' back the long way.

Seeing's how he was coming around when you-all lit a shuck
from Miz Minnie's private office,* then you can bet your last
Yankee dime he'd reason for it."

"You mean they might really have been after Mr. Torreson?"
the financier inquired, looking from the small Texan—having
been equally impressed by the apparent change to his appearance wrought by the force of his personality—to Blood and
back.

"Likely," Clint conceded, despite knowing such was not the
case. "The fact that ole Jubal Branch allowed he wasn't makes
me think it could be. That mother-something son of a bitch
would tell you the sun rose in the west and set in the north,
should doing it serve his ends."

"Was I a praying man," Blood supplemented, once more interrupting his scrutiny of the room in which the interview was
being held, "I'd say Hallelujah to *that.* Nothing 'just happens'
where Jubal Branch's concerned."

"Anyways," Clint drawled, before the plainly indignant Torreson could make a comment, his manner implying there was no
further need for discussion on the subject, "just what do you-all
hope to gain from this *fiesta*?"

"I'm hoping it will bring him to a more amenable frame of
mind," Brickhouse answered, amused by the close to disdainful
way in which the Texans were treating his second in command.
"I'll have all the new men I'll be taking on in view, along with
those here already, as a warning that won't actually be an open
threat or challenge that I'm ready to resist. All the main local
dignitaries I have on the payroll will be here, to act as a re-
minder that I am not without influence in high places. Then I

* "Lit a shuck": A cowhand's expression for "leaving hurriedly." It derives
from the habit in night camps of trail drives and roundups of "shucks"—
dried corn cobs—being available to supply illumination for anybody who
had to leave the firelight and walk in the darkness. As the shuck burned
away quickly, a person had to move fast if wanting to benefit from its light.
*J.T.E.*

# FREE—MAGNIFICENT WALL CALENDAR!
# FREE—PREVIEW OF SACKETT
• No Obligation!  • No Purchase Necessary!

## Yes! I'm claiming my reward!

Send SACKETT for 15 days free! If I keep this volume, I will pay just $10.95 plus shipping and handling. Future Louis L'Amour Westerns will be sent to me about once a month, on a 15-day, Free-Examination basis. I understand that there is no minimum number of books to buy, and I may cancel my subscription at any time. The Free Louis L'Amour wall calendar is mine to keep even if I decide to return SACKETT.

"WANTED!"
STICKER
GOES HERE

NAME _____

ADDRESS _____

CITY _____

STATE _____ ZIP _____

## MY NO RISK GUARANTEE:

There's no obligation to buy. The free calendar is mine to keep. I may preview SACKETT and any other Louis L'Amour book for 15 days. If I don't want it, I simply return the book and owe nothing. If I keep it, I pay only $10.95 (plus postage and handling).

IL2

70136

# Track down and capture exciting western adventure from one of America's foremost novelists!

- It's free! • No obligation! • Exclusive value!

will agree to pay him a slight, face-saving, increase; but on the clear understanding that any further raises are out of the question."

"Once we've got the extra guns, I'd tell him to go to hell and whistle for any more payments!" Torreson growled, looking to the Texans—although Blood was gazing at the paintings on the walls rather than showing any further interest in the conversation. "Wouldn't you?"

"Only happen I wanted a shooting war straightaway, or at least a whole heap of grief on my hands later," Clint replied. "Because any time you threaten a greaser, or call him down with no way of saving face should he want to back out, then, *mister,* you've got trouble on your hands."

"That's what *I've* said all along!" the financier asserted. However, having no wish to cause an open clash—at least, not until he had found somebody more competent, if less ambitious, to replace Torreson—he sought for a way to change the potentially dangerous subject and found it by observing the taller Texan. "I see you are admiring my little collection, Mr. Blood."

"You can say *that* again," replied the man in question, having left his seat to make a closer examination of one of the paintings. "I've *never* seen the like of these any other place I've been."

There was justification for the comment.

The room was tastefully and luxuriously furnished after the style to be expected of the *hacienda* of a wealthy Mexican. However, the painting presented an unusual—bizarre even—note in such surroundings. Well executed though each undoubtedly was, the financier's statement indicated he had brought them with him instead of taking them over when purchasing the property. They were all variations upon a single theme. Whether depicting a scene in or out of doors, each was of well-endowed and voluptuous women in various stages of undress—mostly with the clothing torn to the point of immodesty—fighting with one another.

"It's something of a hobby of mine," Brickhouse claimed, also rising and crossing to join Blood in looking at a scene of several town and saloon women engaged in a wild free-for-all in a barroom. "That's 'The Battle at Bearcat Annie's.' Going to the next, which showed a brunette and a blonde, clad only in black tights, participating in a bloody boxing match, he went on. "This is Wild Bill Hickok's wife, Agnes, versus Battling Binnie Gates." Escorting the Texan to the rest in turn, he continued with his explanations of the events being illustrated. "Calamity Jane and Belle Starr at Elkhorn. Freddie Woods and Buffalo Kate Gilgore in Mulrooney. Dawn Sutherland and Barbe de Martin. Madame Moustache and Poker Alice. Belle Boyd's bare-knuckle fight with the professional woman pugilist, English Flo. Calamity Jane and Madame Bulldog, Calamity's only recorded defeat, incidentally, and here she is again, taking on that *Métis* girl who was trying to start an Indian uprising in Canada."

"Whee-dogie!" Blood remarked with a grin. "Wasn't that Calamity Jane the fightingest li'l ole gal?"

"That she was, sir, that she was!" the financier agreed, his fat face registering an enthusiasm mingled with lust. He was pointing to the last of the pictures, which had the two combatants once more wearing nothing except black tights—although locked in a savage, hair-tearing fight—and being watched by an audience of appreciative Mexicans. "So too was the Rebel Spy, by all accounts.* This is of the second fight she had with the Union Secret Service agent, Eve Coniston."**

"Looks like it was one hell of a whirl," the Texan com-

---

* There is nothing in the records of Alvin Dustine "Cap" Fog to suggest from where Albert Brickhouse obtained his information upon this subject. *J.T.E.*

** The two meetings between Belle "the Rebel Spy" Boyd and Eve Coniston are recorded in *The Bloody Border* and *Back to the Bloody Border.* *J.T.E.*

mented. "How come I've never seen any paintings like this around 'n' about?"

"I commissioned them all personally," Brickhouse explained with pride, then his expression changed to annoyance as he swung his gaze from the painting to Torreson. "And I was hoping to dupli—" The buzzing of the telephone that had been installed since he had moved into the *hacienda* brought the words to an end. After crossing to the desk, he picked up the earpiece and, after listening for a moment, said, "Yes, this is he — Ah, my dear Miss Lassiter, I was meaning to call you."

# 9

# ARE YOU *STILL* LOOKING FOR A FIGHT

"Miz Minnie wants to see you-all in her office straightaway!"

Sitting on the bed of her small room, Rita Ansell fingered her forehead gingerly as she listened to the girl who had just arrived. Much of its earlier throbbing had gone and an examination in the mirror on her dressing table showed only a slight reddening. Clearly Minnie Lassiter knew exactly how much force to apply, so that she stunned the fighters without leaving bruising, or causing them more serious damage than a headache on regaining consciousness.

"What for?" the brunette inquired without rising.

"You'll find out soon enough," the messenger replied. Although she had not been informed of the reason for the summons, she could have made a shrewd guess why it was sent. Instead of saying anything about that, she went on in a tone of urgency mingled with concern for the other's welfare. "Come on. After what's been happening, she's madder than a scalded cat. Was I you-all, I wouldn't keep her waiting."

"What's made her so mad?" Rita inquired, standing up and

reaching for the diaphanous pale-blue silk negligee that she had not waited to put on before she had gone downstairs to try to retrieve the stockings stolen by the buxom red-haired prostitute.

"There was some trouble after she'd knocked you and Daisy Extall out," the girl explained, a natural tendency to gossip overriding the desire to carry out the duty she had been given. "First those three fellers who'd been drinking with Daisy got licked in a fight with Rapido Clint—"

"Who?" Rita put in, the name having been spoken in a way that implied it belonged to a well-known person. She drew on the negligee and left it unfastened.

"A famous and badly wanted outlaw from up Fort Worth way," the girl answered, although she had never heard of Clint before that afternoon. "Surely you must have heard of *him*?"

"I'm afraid I haven't," the brunette confessed with a smile, going to the dressing table and taking a pair of stockings from the top drawer. "Don't forget, I only arrived in Texas recently. What happened then?"

"He beat the three of them easy," the girl declared. "And, when Miz Minnie tried to teach him a lesson by kneeing him in the balls while they were shaking hands, like she always does to anybody who starts a fight, he stopped her as if he'd been expecting it. The Rangers arrived before the Garnell boys could get at him. But before they sent him and another feller away, she tried to kick him. Although he was handcuffed, he grabbed her leg and threw her across the room. Why, if Gloria Deak and me hadn't stopped her, she might have hurt herself, way he did it. Which shows you how *good* he is, doing such twice to Miz Minnie. *Nobody* else had *ever* done anything like it."

"It looks as if I missed some excitement," Rita remarked, drawing the conclusion that the madam of the Premier Chicken Ranch must be well liked to evoke such a sympathetic response from one of its prostitutes.

"It didn't end there," the girl stated. "That old Sergeant

Branch made Miz Minnie let him and his men wait here in case
Comanche Blood, Rapido Clint's sidekick, came here as well."

"Did he come?" Rita asked, coupling the stocking she had
drawn on her left leg to the straps of the garter belt she wore
under her panties.

"No. He rescued them and they shot the Ranger who was
taking them to the jailhouse in El Paso."

"Them?"

"Rapido Clint and the man who'd been in Miz Minnie's office."

"Which man was that?"

"I dunno who he was, I've never seen him here before," the
girl replied, then cocked her head toward the door to listen to
the sound of passing feet. Remembering why she was visiting
the brunette, she went on in a similarly urgent tone to that she
had employed on her arrival. "Come on. That's Daisy Extall on
her way down now—"

"Is it?" Rita said coldly, starting to rise with a grim expression coming to her face. "Well, I'll just go—"

"Leave her be, if you value your hide!" The girl gasped, showing alarm.

"She *doesn't* frighten *me!*" Rita asserted, taking a step forward.

"It's not *her* you should be worried about!" the girl warned,
catching the brunette by the arm and stopping her. "If you go
making fuss again, Miz Minnie'll give you the licking of your
life."

"Do you think she *can*?" Rita inquired.

"I *know* she can!" the girl corrected. "You should have seen
the way she took Daisy Extall, and Daisy's not the first. Miz
Minnie's the best madam I've ever had, but she doesn't take sass
from *anybody,* and those who've tried to give it soon got to be
sorry they had. So leave Daisy be. It's for your own good.
Maybe you'll get your chance to tangle with her later."

"I intend to!" the brunette declared. "This place isn't big enough for the two of us and I'm not meaning to leave."

"That's exactly what *she* said just now when I told her Miz Minnie wanted to see you both," the girl remarked. "Are you ready?"

"I am," Rita confirmed, having put on the other stocking while talking. "Let's go. And thanks for the warning. I'll keep all you've told me in mind."

In spite of the final sentence, the brunette was filled with a sense of disappointment and annoyance as she accompanied the other girl down to the ground floor. From what she had heard, the events of the afternoon that had followed her abortive fight with the redhead could have ruined the end toward which she was working.

Although Rita was clearly of great interest to them, none of the other employees of the brothel who was in the reception room offered to speak. Instead, they watched in silence as she crossed to where Daisy—having knocked and been bidden to enter—was opening the door of Minnie Lassiter's office. On going in, despite having looked back and seen the brunette approaching, the redhead closed the door behind her. Restraining her feelings over such behavior, Rita obtained permission to follow Daisy in. They glowered at each other, but neither addressed the other nor offered to resume their earlier conflict.

"What started it?" the madam inquired bluntly, standing behind her desk and refraining from offering the girls a seat, as she would have done if the forthcoming interview had been of a nondisciplinary nature.

"She did!" Daisy accused, aware of the lack of hospitality entailed and gesturing toward the brunette.

"Only because you stole those stockings from *me*!" Rita countered, indicating the black silk coverings of the redhead's plump legs.

"I only *borrowed* them!" Daisy claimed, cheeks reddening, but kept her temper under control.

"Like hell you did!" Rita contradicted indignantly, clenching her fists.

"That's *enough!*" Minnie snapped as the two girls faced each other like a pair of bobcats meeting on a narrow track. However, seeing the sullen-faced redhead losing the aggressive attitude and, remembering the warning from the messenger, the brunette also lowered her clenched fists. Once this happened, the madam went on in her usual tone. "It seems you two can't get on with one another."

"I don't get on with *thieves* at any time, Miss Minnie!" Rita asserted.

"If you ask me," Daisy complained, "she's just looking for a fight."

"Are you *still* looking for a fight, Miss Ansell?" the madam inquired, almost gently.

"Any time that overstuffed old bitch wants one!" the brunette declared. "Because I mean to have my stockings back!"

"Well, Miss Extall?" Minnie asked, far from displeased by the way in which the conversation was going.

"She can have the mother-something stockings back," Daisy replied. "Any time she can take them off me!"

"Well, Miss Ansell?" Minnie hinted.

"I'll take them back *now,* Miss Minnie!" the brunette answered, combining a respectful attitude toward the madame with a grim determination. "Or any time *you* want me to."

"How does that strike *you,* Miss Extall?" Minnie wanted to know.

"Just you let her *try* any time that suits you, Miss Minnie!" confirmed the redhead, knowing what was coming.

"Very well," the madam said, showing none of the satisfaction she was feeling. "As neither of you appears to be willing to accept conciliation to keep peace here, I'll arrange for you to settle your differences the way *you're* determined it will happen."

"When?" Rita asked eagerly.

"On Saturday," Minnie answered.

"*Saturday?*" Rita repeated, looking disappointed.

"On Saturday," Minnie confirmed.

"In the bar—reception room?" the brunette inquired, making the substitution as she remembered that the madam disliked having the lesser name employed.

"In *Mexico,*" Minnie corrected.

"Not that I care where I thrash the life out of this overstuffed bitch," Rita said, still employing a mixture of politeness and deference. "But why *Mexico* instead of here?"

"For the best possible of reasons, Miss Ansell," Minnie replied, studying the brunette speculatively and concluding that curiosity rather than concern had prompted the question. "There is a gentleman who owns a *hacienda* not far from Juarez. One of his pleasures is to watch women fight. So, as you two are clearly incompatible and I see no way in which you-all will become compatible until this matter is settled, I feel we should take advantage of his offer."

"What offer is that, please?" Rita queried, but politely and showing interest rather than disinclination.

"He has asked that I bring two of my young ladies, preferably who have a disagreement to resolve, to a *fiesta* he is giving for certain prominent Mexican businessmen on Saturday evening," Minnie explained. "They are to settle their differences before an all-male audience. To ensure they do not disappoint the spectators, he is offering a purse of five hundred dollars; to be divided four hundred for the winner and the other hundred for the loser."

"Why not winner takes *all*?" Rita suggested, throwing a look filled with challenge at the redhead.

"I'm for *that*!" Daisy seconded savagely. "And the loser gets the shit away from here!"

"Very well," the madam assented, being aware that to keep two such obviously incompatible girls under the same roof could mean a constant threat of trouble between them and the disruption of the rest of the staff who would be taking sides. "If that is the way you want it?"

"That's just the way I want it!" Daisy affirmed, making clutching motions with her fingers and clearly anticipating the forthcoming fracas.

"I wouldn't have it any *other* way," Rita replied, but without any dramatic or threatening gestures.

"Very well, *ladies,*" Minnie said, looking from the brunette to the redhead and back. "As you are in accord, that is the way it will be." She paused, then her voice took on a timbre charged with warning as she continued. "You can go now and I trust neither of you will attempt to cause a further scene, such as that disgusting example of behavior in the reception room, before Saturday. To do so will incur my severe displeasure. In fact, I feel *neither* of you should appear there between now and our departure on Saturday."

"But that will mean I don't turn any tricks!" Rita protested.

"And *me!*" Daisy went on.

"I'm afraid you have only yourselves to blame for *that,*" Minnie pointed out. "And it will give you each an added incentive to win on Saturday. Leave the stockings with me, Miss Extall, then run along, both of you, and bear in mind what I've just said."

A smile played on the madam's face as she watched the girls taking their departure—the redhead now bare-legged—studiously ignoring each other like a pair of earlier-day duelists who had chanced to meet between the challenge and the confrontation upon the field of honor.

From her experiences in the past, Minnie was aware of just how disruptive an influence a feud between two such obviously determined protagonists could be upon the smooth running and business of a brothel. With the other employees and, frequently, the clients taking sides, there was always the threat of it erupting into a battle royal. So she was delighted to have received a proposition that would not only allow the main antagonists to settle their differences without the danger of damage to the furnishings and fittings, but was offering her a bonus of at least five hundred dollars. She had already had a "purse" of a thousand dollars stipulated, but hoped to persuade the maker to raise the ante.

With the latter thought in mind, Minnie sat down and took the earpiece of the telephone on the desk from its hook.

"I want to place a call to Mr. Brickhouse, at the *Hacienda Naranja* in Juarez, please," the madam requested, after her jiggling of the hook had attracted the attention of an operator in the telephone exchange at El Paso. On being connected, she continued, "I've obtained the 'merchandise' you requested, but I'm afraid it will be more expensive than you-all offered. Fifteen hundred dollars is the *absolute* minimum *they* will accept. Yes, I'm certain it will be worthwhile. If not, you don't need to pay. Is that satisfactory? It is? Very well, I will have the 'merchandise' delivered on Saturday before six o'clock in the evening."

Hanging up the earpiece, Minnie lounged back in her chair with an expansive smile. All in all, providing the two girls gave the satisfactory performance she felt sure would be forthcoming, the day showed signs of being quite profitable. Furthermore, she now had the opportunity of following Rapido Clint and Comanche Blood who, she had ascertained during her earlier call, were at the *Hacienda Naranja*. She wanted to learn more about their backgrounds and to see whether they would be of any use to Hogan Turtle.

Having left the office, unaware of the fact that the madam was defrauding the winner of a thousand dollars, Rita watched Daisy joining some of the other girls. As on their arrival in the reception room, everybody was clearly eager to learn what had taken place during the interview. Remembering the advice they had been given, although *orders* would be a more apt description, Rita decided to let the redhead satisfy their curiosity.

Going up the stairs to her room, the brunette considered the situation with mixed emotions. She had brought about a state of affairs that in fact she required, but she wondered if she could attain her end. And, having done so, would she be able to carry out the rest of her intentions?

Thinking of why she had embarked upon such a course, Rita told herself she not only *could,* but *would*!

# 10
# HE'S MADE A SUCKER OUT OF YOU

"Ah, here you are, Mr. Clint, Mr. Blood!" Albert Brickhouse greeted jovially, rising from his place at one end of the well-laid table in the main dining room of the *Hacienda Naranja*. "Come in, gentlemen, come in. I trust you are finding your accommodation to your complete satisfaction."

"It surely is for *me*," the dark Texan declared. As his companion nodded in agreement, he continued. "I know ole Rapido here has, but I've for sure never been given the chance to sleep in nothing so fancy."

After completing the telephone conversation with Minnie Lassiter, which had put him in an even better mood than when he was exhibiting his collection of unconventional works of art to Comanche Blood, the financier had yielded to Victor Torreson's hints and settled down to resume the interrupted discussion. He had given further evidence of his shrewdness by commenting upon the fact that, despite frequently employing the jargon of cowhands and criminals, Rapido Clint also spoke in the manner of one who had had a good background and supe-

rior education to that of his companion. Although the small
Texan had admitted to being the black sheep of a well-to-do
family, he had refused to supply any further details. In fact, he
had stated bluntly that he would take the gravest exception to
any attempts to pry into the matter.

Accepting the warning and changing the subject with either
real or well-simulated amiability, Brickhouse had offered to employ the two young Texans to help reinforce his guard. There
had been a brief debate upon the matter of how much money
they would receive for their services. The sum was settled, but it
had been at a somewhat lower figure than was suggested by
Clint. Countering the demand, the financier had pointed out
that not only might there be no actual danger involved, but they
would have all their food, liquor, such arms and ammunition as
they required, and accommodation provided for as long as they
stayed at the *Hacienda Naranja*. On those points having been
conceded and the deal concluded, Torreson had taken them upstairs to their quarters.

As Blood had intimated, the two young men would have been
very hard to please if they had not been satisfied with the accommodation to which they were allocated. They were put into
adjoining rooms, with a sturdy connecting balcony that would
offer adequate protection and a reasonably safe firing point in
the event of an attack. While not as luxurious as those of the
library, dining room, and, they suspected, the financier's quarters, the furnishings were clean and comfortable. There was
only one point to which they had taken exception. While the
doors had bolts on the inside, there was no way they could be
locked from the outside when the occupants were not present.

On showing the Texans in, Torreson had commented that the
double beds would be useful when, as frequently happened, girls
were brought in from Juarez to entertain those of the fighting
force who were not on guard duty. At the pair's request, he had
supplied Clint with a Winchester model of 1894 carbine. To
augment his Holland & Holland .357 magnum sporting rifle—

which was far from ideal for shooting rapidly or at shorter ranges—Blood had selected a trench gun. Asked if he would care for a handgun, he had replied that he had never gained any proficiency with one and preferred to rely on his hunting knife for fighting at close quarters.

Although the fugitive from New York had told the two Texans what time to come downstairs for dinner, they had discovered that—with the exception of the four men who were keeping watch at the gates—the rest of the guard force had already assembled and were seated.

Walking through the open double doors and across the dining room, Clint and Blood studied their surroundings. Between Brickhouse and Torreson, who was occupying the seat at the other end, there were four men on each side of the table. Their ages ranged from one who could be in his early twenties to a couple who looked to be at least approaching their fifties. While they were wearing different styles of clothing, one thing each had in common was that he had on a gunbelt with a revolver or an automatic pistol in its holster. Another similarity was the hardness of their faces and the cold, watchful wariness of their eyes. Furthermore, they were alike in subjecting the new arrivals to a scrutiny just as keen as they were receiving and taking note that, apart from the hunting knife on Blood's belt, neither showed any sign of being armed.

To experienced eyes, the signs were plain. For all their comparative youth, the eyes of Rapido Clint and Comanche Blood were very experienced!

From their examination, the two Texans deduced the nature of the company with whom they would be mixing. It was not one in which a newcomer would be advised to display a meek or subservient demeanor. Or to try to assert himself too forcefully unless ready, willing, and competent to back his play to the hilt.

Except for the financier, every man at the table belonged to that stratum of criminal society that supplied the "muscle" required for a robbery or other illegal enterprise. Their specialty would be to provide brawn, or skill with and a willingness to use firearms, rather than intelligence and finesse. In the days of the Old West, they would have belonged to the category known as *pistoleros,* or "hired guns," and they were currently finding employment in a similar capacity.

"Please come and sit on either side of me, Mr. Clint, Mr. Blood," Brickhouse offered as the Texans approached the table. "Then, before dinner is served, I will introduce you to the rest of these gentlemen."

*"Gracias,"* Clint replied, having noticed that the seats immediately to the right and left of the financier were unoccupied.

While speaking, the small Texan took the nearer chair. Raising no complaint, Blood continued to stroll around and sat on the other side.

"So you're this here real tough, Ranger-shooting Rapido Clint's Vic there's allowing to be all wool and a yard wide. Can't say's I've *ever* heard of you."

The comment, delivered in a derisively challenging tone with a North Texas accent, came from the youngest of the assembled hardcases. Dressed in the dandified clothes affected by rodeo competitors, which were grubby through neglect rather than because they had been worn while he was working, he was tall and well built. Brown-haired and moderately good-looking, there was an arrogance about his demeanor that warned of a truculent and bullying nature.

The speaker was sitting three places below Blood and next to the oldest of the men around the table. From the way in which they and the other two occupants of that side were positioned, it was apparent that there was some connection between them.

Also dressed after the fashion of the range country, albeit in a less flamboyant and more functional style, the oldest man was of something over medium height and of stocky build. Gray-haired and heavily mustached, he had a leathery and inscrutable face. He conveyed the impression of knowing he was tough, but he did not have the young man's self-assertive bombast.

Somewhat taller and slimmer than the elderly man, which did not make them puny, the remaining pair on Blood's side were sufficiently alike and resembled him enough to suggest they were his twin sons. They were dressed in much the same fashion too, and looked tough but not overbright.

"I've likely never heard of *you* either, comes to that," Clint replied, reversing direction before he sat down and letting his left hand go to the left lapel of the waist-length brown leather jacket. "And Mr. Torreson didn't tell you right. I don't just restrict myself to shooting *Rangers.*"

"What's *that* supposed to mean?" the young man challenged, starting to rise and then hesitating as he was subjected to the apparent metamorphosis created by the force of the small Texan's personality when subjected to threatening behavior.

"Leave be, Claude!" snapped the eldest hardcase as, acting with commendable speed and strength, he caught hold and jerked down the speaker. Then, looking at Clint speculatively, he continued in an even tone that showed he too originated from North Texas. "Young 'n didn't mean nothing by what he said, friend. Ain't no call to get riled."

"I'm not *riled,* mister," the small Texan answered, sitting down again. "I'm not looking for trouble either, but I won't back off from it so much as a short step should *anybody* figure on trying me out."

"Come, gentlemen, come!" Brickhouse put in hastily, a somewhat alarmed timbre underlying the clearly forced joviality. Ringing the small silver bell that was next to the ashtray he was using, he went on. "Let's have the glasses filled while I introduce our new companions."

Still showing concern after a decanter that proved to be filled with bourbon was circulated, the financier performed the introductions. The elderly man was Turk Laker and the pair with the family resemblance, his twin sons, Matthew and Luke, the young hardcase being his nephew, Claude Bigelow. It was obvious to Clint and Blood that the other four—Hank Wade, Earl

Newton, Will Granger and Cyrus Kenover—formed a separate clique and had found the brief, abortive confrontation more amusing than disturbing.

Despite the inauspicious way in which it had commenced, the meal served by the Mexican domestic staff proved to be plain fare, but of good quality and more than adequate quantity. Although the decanter was kept replenished and in continuous use, neither Brickhouse nor the two newcomers partook of its contents to the extent of the rest of the men. In fact, while the financier drank enough to bring a flush to his cheeks and lose his earlier concern, Clint and Blood did hardly more than sip at the second fillings of their glasses.

Despite Bigelow sitting in sullen silence and glowering at the cause of his discomfiture, a lively conversation was carried out during the meal. It was clear that everybody found the newcomers of great interest. There was some probing, intended to learn more about them, but it was kept within the bounds allowed by their unwritten code. Speaking amiably and showing no animosity, Turk Laker requested information about a reliable fence in the Dallas-Fort Worth area. After giving a name, Clint said he and Blood only took money or items they intended for their own use from their victims as this removed the risks involved in dealing with a professional buyer of stolen goods. Having recently completed a five-year prison sentence as a result of being betrayed by a fence, Kenover brought a laugh by stating he wished he had shown such good sense.

"Hey, boss!" Torreson called, taking advantage of a lull in the conversation after the meal was over and coffee was being served. "Do you reckon Mr. Clint could set fire to a sugar lump like you do?"

"Well, now!" Brickhouse said, the momentary suggestion of eagerness he began to show dying away as he turned his gaze to the small Texan.

"Hey, yeah!" Luke Laker exclaimed. Bigelow, however—despite appearing on the point of speaking—did not break his surly silence. "I'll bet he wouldn't be no better at doing it than any of us was!"

"Bet!" the small Texan drawled. "Did I hear you-all say something about a *bet*?"

"Yeah," Luke confirmed. "That's *just* what you heard me say something about."

"You don't mean a bet for *money*?" Clint suggested, in a manner redolent of eagerness.

"I wouldn't know about anybody else here," Luke asserted, with the air of one employing a witticism. "But I don't have a whole heap of use for glass beads 'n' trade cloth."

"That sounds like it could've been pointed at *me*!" Blood said with a growl, making almost his first contribution to the conversation since entering the dining room.

"It *wasn't*, I assure you!" Brickhouse declared in the silence that fell after the softly spoken and yet somehow menacing words. His manner was placatory. He directed his next words to Clint, before the potential source of contention could be continued. "Mr. Torreson is referring to a simple little contest, sir. It all revolves around whether you, or I, can set alight a cube of sugar."

"Set alight a cube of sugar?" the small Texan repeated, glancing at the bowl filled with the objects in question.

"That is what it's all about, sir," the financier answered, his manner suggesting the matter was a foregone conclusion.

"*You* can set fire to a sugar cube, sir?" Clint inquired.

"I frequently have," Brickhouse admitted, his hesitant and placatory air being replaced by one of confident assurance.

"And you're saying I *can't*?" Clint went on.

"All I'm saying is that the knack of doing it is one very few people possess," Brickhouse corrected.

"Well, now," Clint drawled, his bearing filled with self-confidence. "For all my daddy said I should never show I can do *anything* as well as the *boss*, I reckon I can do her if she can be done."

"You-all still wanting to bet on it?" Luke asked eagerly.

"I just reckon I *might* at that," Clint replied, reaching with his left hand to take the wallet from his jacket's inside right pocket. "There's fifteen hundred li'l ole iron men in this says I can do it, if anybody else can."

"I'll take fifty of that!" Bigelow offered.

"Cash on the barrelhead, *hombre*!" Clint warned, his manner offensive. "Cover what's put down, Comanch', up to the fifteen hundred."

"Simmer down and put your money up, Cousin Claude!" Luke ordered, nudging the indignant young man in the ribs to prevent his intended angry comment. "I'll go for fifty of it, Comanch'."

"And me!" Matthew seconded, joining his brother in producing sufficient money to form their respective stakes.

Although Turk Laker refrained and Bigelow proved to have only half the amount he had proposed, the rest of the guards and Torreson each put up a sum of money. For all the pay they were receiving, however, when they were finished, Blood had used only a thousand of Clint's dollars to cover their bets.

"How about you-all, sir?" the small Texan inquired, looking at the financier.

"I'll take the r—" Brickhouse began, but the avaricious glint in his eyes died away as he looked from the depleted pile of money to its owner and he continued in a less eager tone. "To show you how confident I am, I'll lay—five hundred against two hundred and fifty from you that *you* can't set fire to the cube with a match, but I can."

"Why not put up a grand against my five hundred?" Clint suggested.

"I'd rather not," Brickhouse replied, after a moment's hesitation that implied he was struggling to refrain from accepting the offer.

"You're the boss, sir," Clint declared cheerfully. "And I'll take a draw on your five hundred. Pass along that bowl in front of you-all, Earl, so's I can give her a whirl."

"That's real poetry, Rapido." Tall, lanky, middle-age Earl Newton grinned, doing as requested although there was another sugar bowl much closer to the small Texan.

"Here we go," Clint said, digging into the bowl and selecting one of the cubes from near the bottom. Turning it over between his fingers, he interrupted his inspection to glance at the financier and went on. "No offense meant, sir, but you-all don't mind if I use *my* matches?"

"Certainly not," Brickhouse assented cheerfully, returning the box he had taken from his pocket. Offering a fountain pen to Rapido, he continued. "To make sure all is fair and aboveboard, mark one side of the cube."

After waving aside the pen, Clint produced the stub of an indelible pencil from the left breast pocket of his jacket and made a rough pentagon shape on one surface of the sugar cube. He dropped the pencil onto the table, then extracted the items required for the experiment from the right side pocket of his Levi's. Striking a match, he applied the flame to a corner of the cube at the opposite side to the mark he had made. However, all that resulted was the formation of a brown and molasseslike mess.

"Well, I'll be damned!" Clint declared in exasperation, shaking out the flame as it threatened to burn his fingers without having produced the desired effect. "If you-all can get that goddamned thing to burning, sir, I'll give you best on it."

"One can try," Brickhouse answered with a disarming gesture that was intended to suggest he believed the end was still in doubt. After placing the cigar he was smoking on the partially filled ashtray, he moved to where his plate had been during the meal.

"With *my* matches!" Clint ordered rather than suggested, handing over the charred cube.

"Of course, sir," the financier agreed without hesitation or apparent annoyance. "And, to assure you there is no subterfuge, will you light and hand it to me, please?"

"Why, sure," Clint drawled, realizing that to do so would reduce the time in which the match could be held to the sugar. He glanced down as he removed another from his box.

Watched by everybody around the table, all but Clint and Blood grinning in eager expectation, Brickhouse accepted the lighted match. After raising the cube from where he had been holding it above the ashtray, he applied the flame to the charred area. Almost immediately, a red glow arose and the cube caught alight.

"Well, I'll be *damned*!" The small Texan gasped, staring as if unable to believe the evidence of his eyes. "If that doesn't beat *all*!"

"Make sure it is the same cube you used, sir," the financier requested, clearly still intending to remove any suggestion of subterfuge as he shook out the flame.

"That's my mark, all right!" Clint confirmed, having carried out the inspection. He shook his head and looked perplexed.

"Looks like you're not's goddamned slick's you reckoned!" Bigelow scoffed, ignoring the fact that he too had failed in a similar attempt, as he snatched up his winnings with both hands. "He's made a sucker out of you!"

"There's some would say whoever sired you did worse than that to your mother," Clint replied coldly. "Or did she always want a big-mouthed yack to pass off as a son?"

"God damn you!" Bigelow spat out, dropping the money and starting to thrust himself from the table with the intention of rising and drawing his gun.

Instantly Clint also shoved his seat backward; but with a difference. He did not attempt to stand up before commencing to arm himself. While his left hand rose to grasp and draw open the near side of the jacket, the right flashed over to disappear briefly beneath it. Grasping the butt of the Colt Government model .45 automatic pistol, he twisted it forward. Liberated from the spring-retention clips of the shoulder holster that had been in his bedroll and was so well designed there had been no sign of the weapon's presence upon his person, it came into view. With his thumb thrusting down the manual safety catch, the hammer being in the fully cocked position, he pointed the barrel in the young man's direction.

Startled by the speed with which the big black automatic appeared, and alarmed over the realization of his own unreadiness to fight back, Bigelow tried to complete standing up and also to move away from the danger. Overturning the chair in his haste, he tripped and toppled backward. On landing, breaking the chair beneath him, his head struck the floor and he was stunned by the impact.

"It's between him and me, gents!" Clint claimed in an even tone, his weapon not moving from the empty space left vacant by the young man's disappearance. He swung his gaze from Turk Laker to each of the twin brothers in turn. "Unless you feel called upon to take up for him, that is."

"Can't say's we do," the old man answered, without so much as a glance for confirmation or concurrence from his sons. "Young Claude's got hisself a real bad habit of talking out of turn." Looking over his shoulder, he went on. "Maybe that crack on the head he's took'll knock some sense into him. Take him up to his room, boys, 'n' see he stays up there when he comes to."

Looking resentful but making no argument, the brothers did as they were told. After they had departed carrying the unconscious Bigelow between them, Clint returned the Colt to its holster. He apologized to Brickhouse for the disturbance, while the other men were picking up their money. Then conversation welled up around the table, but with no reference to either the bet or its aftermath.

Just before midnight, having taken part in a poker game in which he won back most of his money by his shrewd play, Clint went upstairs with Blood. After going past his companion's room, he reached his own door and glanced upward.

"Good night, Comanch'," the small Texan called. "I surely hope we don't get disturbed before morning."

Then he opened the door. Although he had left the light on when he went downstairs, it was extinguished. Nor did the bulb respond when he tried the switch. However, satisfied there was sufficient illumination given by the perimeter lights outside, he walked in and closed the door behind him.

Waiting until their intended victim was halfway to the bed, having stood in the shadows on the hinged side of the door after removing the light bulb from its socket, the Laker brothers moved forward. They had removed their boots as an aid to silence. Arriving without making any noise, each caught hold of one of his arms.

"We've got the bastard, Claude!" Matthew announced quietly, clapping one hand over the small Texan's mouth to stifle any outcry.

Instantly Bigelow thrust open the door of the big wardrobe in which he had been hiding. The faint light from the closed French windows glinted dully on the brass knuckles he wore on his right hand as he darted forward.

# 11
# THERE'S NO DARK MEAT
# IN *THAT* FAMILY

Although they were acting without the knowledge and approval
of their father, who generally supplied whatever thinking was
needed where their various nefarious activities were concerned,
the Laker brothers had no complaints about the way in which
the scheme concocted by Claude Bigelow was working. Even
Matthew, the elder of the twins by about twenty minutes, had
lost his earlier pessimism and was convinced that everything
was progressing in a satisfactory manner.

When he had recovered from the effects of the fall and been
told that he and his cousins were ordered by his "Uncle Turk"
to remain upstairs instead of returning to the dining room, Bigelow had suggested that they should avenge the insult placed
upon the honor of the family. Always the more easily led, despite Matthew being dubious, Luke had been in agreement with
the plan put forward by the younger man. The fact that everything so far had gone as he had claimed it would had done much
to persuade even the older brother that the rest of their plan
would prove equally successful.

The absence of locks on the doors of the upstairs rooms, except for those occupied by Albert Brickhouse, had allowed the conspirators to gain unimpeded admittance to Rapido Clint's quarters. All that had remained to be done was remove the electric light bulb and wait for him to come up. As the scheme had not been hatched and put into operation until a quarter to twelve, they were not required to remain for long in the semi-darkness before their quarry arrived. What was more, the small Texan had made it easy for them to know he was coming by speaking in a loud voice to Comanche Blood before opening the door and entering.

Having caught Clint by the arms and with Matthew's right hand covering his mouth to prevent him from summoning the Texan to his aid, the brothers anticipated no difficulty in holding him helpless while their cousin inflicted a savage beating with the knuckleduster.

In spite of the twins' optimistic point of view, they very quickly discovered that the task upon which they were engaged was far from being the snap they imagined.

On feeling himself being grasped from either side, Clint responded with rapidity. Instead of trying to extricate himself from their hands, the small Texan allowed his captors to take his weight and support him. By doing so, he was able to devote his whole attention to the most immediate threat to his well-being. Before a blow from the brass knuckles could even be launched at him, he tilted his torso to the rear and brought his lower body forward and upward. After flexing his legs as they were rising, he straightened them vigorously and sent the soles of his boots into the center of the advancing Claude's chest. As his would-be assailant was hurled backward across the room to fall on to the bed, he returned his feet to the ground. However, despite their surprise at the way in which Clint had acted, the brothers still held him. If anything, they were gripping him even more tightly.

Deciding that Matthew posed the lesser threat, his right arm being grasped by only one hand, Clint gave a sudden jerk at the restraint upon it. As he was pulling, he raised and drove back his left foot in a stamping kick that scraped down the front of the elder brother's right shin. Letting out a howl of pain, Matthew let go of Clint's arm and face and staggered away from him.

Despite the fact that Bigelow was sitting up and that he had liberated his right arm, the small Texan did not try to bring the Colt Government model .45 automatic pistol from its shoulder holster. Instead, exhibiting a speed similar to that which he had used in the dining room, his free hand went to the right hip pocket of his Levi's and extracted the round-ended stick that had served him so well at Minnie Lassiter's Premier Chicken Ranch. It was to prove equally efficacious against his current assailant.

Applying a surging swing with his trapped arm, Clint hauled Luke forward. Before the younger brother could try to resist, the rounded end protruding ahead of the small Texan's fist drove with considerable force into his solar plexus. Instantly, all the air in Luke's lungs was expelled to form a croak of agony. Snatching free his hands, he stumbled backward and folded at the middle like a pocketknife being closed. After tumbling to the floor, he writhed in torment for a few seconds. Then he went limp and lapsed into unconsciousness.

Despite being free from all restraint, Clint still was not out of danger. Still wearing the brass knuckles and rendered even more furious by the treatment he had received, Bigelow was bouncing upright from the bed.

In spite of the pain he was suffering, the elder of the Laker twins was far from incapacitated. However, having experienced the small Texan's surprising strength and witnessed the apparent ease with which his sibling was dealt, Matthew showed no inclination to return to the fray with bare hands. Instead, he was reaching for his holstered Colt Peacemaker.

Concentrating upon their own intentions, neither Matthew nor Bigelow thought it strange that—being in such dire straits—the small Texan made no attempt to shout and inform his companion in the next room that he required help.

The answer was simple: Rapido Clint considered there was no need for him to do so.

Aware of the lack of security posed by there being no lock, the small Texan had taken precautions upon leaving his room. With Comanche Blood duplicating his actions, having been equally cognizant of the situation, he had fastened a piece of dark thread from the top of the door to its jamb. While this would not prevent an unauthorized entry in their absence, it would serve as a warning that one had taken place.

When he had seen the thread was broken, Clint had known his door had been opened since he had left. As there was no indication of Blood's quarters having been treated in the same fashion, he had guessed who was responsible and what was almost certainly intended. Doubting whether any gunplay would be involved, he had alerted his companion to his suspicions and was ready to counter the anticipated attack as he went in.

However, despite the small Texan's assumption, there was no sign of Blood putting in the expected appearance.

With his situation still so critical, Clint could not spare so much as a second to ponder over the possible reasons for his companion's absence.

Once again the Texan gave his attention to Matthew, but for a different motive this time. Earlier the older twin had been the easiest assailant to deal with. Now he was an even more pressing threat than his cousin. Hurt or not he was bringing out his gun with pretty fair speed.

After throwing himself forward in a dive, Clint passed beneath the rising barrel of the Colt without a moment to spare. In fact, so narrow was the margin, Matthew could neither alter his point of aim nor prevent himself from releasing the hammer. He had pulled back the trigger while making his draw, so the single-action mechanism—which required cocking manually before it could function—operated and discharged the uppermost cartridge in the cylinder.

Ignoring the thunder of the shot so close above him and the heat of the muzzle blast that threatened to scorch his leather jacket, the small Texan alighted on Matthew's lowered left hand. With his body at an upward angle, Clint snapped around his right arm. Driven with all the force he could muster, the end of the stick in front of his thumb and forefinger passed between Matthew's spread legs.

Struck in that portion of the masculine anatomy most susceptible to such an attack, the older twin gave out a strangled shriek of sheer, unadulterated torment. The revolver fell unheeded from his grasp as, joining its mate, his right hand flew to the area of the impact. Gaining not the slightest succor from their clasp, he stumbled away from his attacker and collapsed, fainting from the excruciating pain, against the wall.

Alarmed by the sight of his second cousin being rendered unconscious, Bigelow nevertheless felt the situation was far from as desperate as it had been when he had confronted the surprisingly *large* Texan in the dining room. He was on his feet and confident that he could arrive within striking distance before Clint could rise. Having done so, a kick to the head or body ought to produce sufficient damage to let him administer the working over with the brass knuckles he had come to deliver.

Having decided upon his strategy, Bigelow set forward to carry it out.

At that moment, Comanche Blood put in an appearance.

As he took his second step in the small Texan's direction, the young man heard a crash from his rear. A glance informed him that the French windows had been kicked open. Carrying a trench gun in both hands, Blood was entering from the balcony. Spluttering a curse that was more fear than aggression, Bigelow spun around and swung the fist protected by the brass knuckles in the direction of the rapidly approaching, savage-looking newcomer.

Weaving and ducking so the hand and its potentially lethal covering passed over his head, Comanche rammed the muzzle of his trench gun into the pit of his would-be attacker's stomach. Bigelow went into an involuntary retreat and, as his cousin had done when struck by Clint, was compelled to bend forward from the waist. However, he was not permitted to retire without further attention. Acting like one who was highly trained in fighting with a rifle and bayonet, Blood swung around his weapon. Its butt caught the young hardcase's descending and presented jaw, breaking bone and flinging him in a helpless spin into the corner of the room. He was unconscious before his downward slide ended.

Preceded by shouts of alarm, footsteps sounded in the passage. Then the door of Clint's room was thrown open. With the other men from the dining room following them, Victor Torreson and Turk Laker burst in. They came to a halt and the fugitive from New York showed signs of trying to withdraw as hurriedly as he had entered. There was good reason for his reaction. Executing another exceptionally fast draw, the small Texan had swung toward them holding the big Colt automatic.

"We heard a shot!" Torreson exclaimed, trying to keep any trace of trepidation from his voice. "What the hell happened?"

"I found these three here when I came in," Clint replied, indicating the motionless intruders with a sweeping gesture of his left hand.

"What did they want?" Torreson demanded, when no further information was forthcoming. He glanced from one of the Laker boys to the other and their cousin, then back at the cause of their misfortunes.

"I wouldn't know, not having been given a chance to ask," the small Texan answered. "But, going by the brassies on that fancy-dressed Bill-show hand's fist,* I wouldn't want to take bets it was only to ask me around to take a cup of Limey tea."

"You mean they was *laying* for you?" Torreson inquired, sounding as if he could not believe such a contingency was possible.

"Well now, to a half-smart li'l ole Texas boy like me, it kind of looks like they just *could* have been at that," Clint replied, his tone heavily larded with sarcasm. However, it took on a noticeably more polite timbre as he made it plain he was addressing the remainder of his comment to the father of his two victims. "I *know* you wasn't in on this fool play they made, sir. Which's why I tried not to hurt your boys too bad. Should they feel the same, I'll pretend this never happened comes morning." He paused, then continued in a harder manner. "But only where *they're* concerned. That other son of a bitch had crossed me *three* times already, which's *four* times too many. There's just not room in the *Hacienda Naranja* for him and me both. Either he goes—or I go with him!"

"I'm right sorry things worked out the way they did, Mr. Clint," Turk Laker declared as he walked across to the small Texan and Comanche Blood. They were leaving the rear door of the *Hacienda Naranja*'s main building. Laker gestured toward the 1920 Essex Four car in which his sons and nephew, all looking decidedly the worse for their previous night's activities, were disconsolately sitting. "Comes fuss with that greaser son of a bitch, Guevara, which I reckon both of us knows *can't* be got out from under, I'd've admired to stood alongside you gents."

"I don't reckon that, Comanch' here excepted, there's a man I'd rather have with me comes the water's over the willows and

---

* "Bill-show hand": A braggart who is also a fancy dresser. Derived from the attire worn by performers in the Wild West shows such as were made popular by William Frederick "Buffalo Bill" Cody (1846–1917) during the late 1800s. *J.T.E.*

rising, which I conclude it soon will be," Rapido Clint replied, employing an old trail-driving term for a dangerous situation derived from encountering a badly flooded river while moving a herd of cattle overland on the hoof. "And I don't see why you-all need to pull out."

There had not been a great deal more discussion, apart from Laker having disclaimed all knowledge of his sons' and nephew's intentions, the previous night. On Clint apologizing to Albert Brickhouse for the damage inflicted upon his room's French windows, he had been assured that Comanche Blood's actions were entirely justifiable under the circumstances. With that point settled, the small Texan had requested the removal of the unconscious trio so he could go to bed.

Having slept late that morning, which he and Blood had discovered to be the trait of the hardcases hired to guard the *Hacienda Naranja,* Clint had found several of his future associates present in the dining room when they arrived for breakfast. They had been informed that the Lakers and Claude Bigelow—the latter requiring expert medical attention to fix his broken jaw—were leaving. Going to attend to their horses, the Texans had been accosted by the elderly hardcase.

"I figure it's for the best," Laker claimed. "Young Claude's not about to forget nor forgive what you done to him. Which I don't want him, being kin—even though his momma married a worthless no-account son of a bitch—to come to an untimely end for trying to get even."

"So send him off to be taken care of north of the border," Clint suggested. "That way you could stay on here."

"That wouldn't work neither," Laker asserted regretfully. "You hurt my boys' feelings, long of other things they've got, over what you done, being so small—happen you-all don't take offense at it being mentioned!"

"I don't," the small Texan affirmed. "Way *you're* meaning it, that is."

"Well, that being a fact, my boys're right mortified they got whupped so easy by you," Laker explained. "Could be, some-time when I wasn't on hand to keep a watch over 'em, one or t'other'd get liquored and try to set it to rights. And, well's I've taught 'em, ain't neither's up to a long country mile good enough to do it."

"*Gracias,*" Clint replied, knowing he was receiving some-thing of an accolade.

"It's the living, breathing truth," Laker stated. "Fact being, way you handle yourself when you're riled puts me in mind of somebody I saw a couple of times when I was some younger. Only I don't reckon, 'spite of what I've been told, you *could* be any kin to *him*. Without meaning no offense to you, there's no dark meat in *that* family."

"Which family would that be?" Blood inquired, when his companion did not speak.

"The Hardins, Fogs, and Blazes, over to Rio Hondo County," Turk answered, watching the small Texan and not the poser of the question.

"That takes in a considerable amount of folks," Clint pointed out, with no particular interest as far as could be discerned from his demeanor. "Which one of them are you thinking about?"

"Colonel Dusty Fog,"* the elderly hardcase answered.

"And *I* put you-all in mind of *him*?" the small Texan scoffed. "Way I've heard all my life, he was close to seven foot tall, at least a yard wide, and blond to boot."

"That's what I've allus been told too," Blood supported. "And, 'though I'm some too young to've ever seen Colonel Dusty, I've run across his son—he's a sheriff of Rio Hondo County an' he's a real big son of a bitch without no argument."

* Details of the background and career of Captain Dustine Edward Mars-den "Dusty" Fog, C.S.A., can be found in various volumes of the *Civil War and Floating Outfit* series. The title Colonel was honorary, being given during the later years of his eventful life as a Texas-style tribute to his ability as a fighting man and a leader. *J.T.E.*

"Could be my old mind's going back on me then," Laker conceded amiably. "Only, like I said, Mr. Clint, you surely put me in mind of him when you're riled up and getting set to move."

"Did you tell Mr. Brickhouse that I did?" Clint inquired in a nonchalant and disinterested fashion.

"Nope," Laker admitted. "Nor Vic Torreson neither. I just now went in to say we was leaving and to pick up our pay. Asked if, the boys being hurt too bad to take work for a spell, they'd be getting a bonus. Mr. Brickhouse allowed that's they hadn't got hurt doing nothing for him, they wouldn't. Which's fair enough according to his lights. So it's only fair 'cording to *mine* that I didn't waste my time in making idle talk to *him*. Would it've worried you-all if I had?"

"I can't see any reason why it should," Clint declared. "Well, this isn't getting our horses tended to. I'm right sorry about what happened last night, Mr. Laker."

"Wasn't your fault, Mr. Clint," the elderly hardcase replied. "A man can't blame you-all for defending yourself. There's no hard feelings's far's I'm concerned, and I'll make sure my boys stay well clear of you from now on."

*"Gracias,"* the small Texan drawled. "Maybe we'll meet again along the trail."

"I'll try to see it *never* happens," Laker asserted. Without offering to elaborate upon the cryptic utterance, he nodded and turned to stroll back in the direction of his vehicle.

# 12

# WE SHOULD TEACH HIM
# A LESSON

"Fetching *you* from Texas doesn't seem like it was any too smart
an idea the way things have gone!" Victor Torreson claimed,
scowling across the dining-room table at Rapido Clint. "God
damn it, you haven't been here for a full day yet and you've
already cost us four good men!"

"What the hell did you-all expect ole Rapido to do when
those three sons of bitches jumped him last night?" Comanche
Blood demanded indignantly, before his companion could reply
to the acrimonious accusation. "Are you saying's how he should
just've stood there and let 'em stomp him half, or closer, to
death? Because, *hombre,* that's what they were fixing to do."

The time was shortly after one o'clock on Friday afternoon.

As Clint and Blood had finished attending to the needs of
their horses, Cyrus Kenover had entered the stables accompanied by two young Mexicans. The hardcase had informed the
Texans that all the horses in the *Hacienda Naranja* were taken
outside the walls during daylight hours and allowed to graze.
On being asked whether they wished to have their mounts in-

cluded, Clint had questioned the advisability and safety of such an arrangement. He was told that, as a result of an agreement between Albert Brickhouse and Cristóbal Guevara, the local *bandidos* were ordered to leave the *hacienda*'s stock alone and the edict had been adhered to. Although the small Texan had still expressed misgivings, he had seen how small a stock of fodder was held on the premises and had yielded to his companion's suggestion that they should let the horses go. As Blood had pointed out, should somebody forget Guevara's instructions, they could always obtain more mounts by the same means through which the four had come into their possession.

While the horses were being driven out of the *hacienda* by the Mexicans, with Kenover explaining that no guards were considered necessary due to the agreement, Clint and Blood had been summoned to the financier. The message was delivered by a small, middle-age, balding, fragile-looking and obsequious white man they had not seen before. Introducing himself as "Wildersleeve, Mr. Brickhouse's valet," he had stated that he did not know why his employer wished to see them.

After being escorted to the left side of the building, the Texans had found the financier standing at the firing point of a temporary firing range. He was shooting a light-caliber revolver, with no success, at a homemade target and requested their advice as to the reason for his failure to make a hit. Showing no hesitation, having suspected he was being put to a test, Clint had given a superlative exhibition of not only how well he could fire his Colt Government model .45 automatic with either hand, but demonstrated the speed with which he could draw it from the shoulder holster and make a hit in the "kill" area of the man-size, man-shaped target at a distance of about seven yards. The sound of the shooting had attracted most of the guard force, and, at the end of his display, the small Texan had known that they were all impressed by his skill.

With the demonstration over, having nothing else to demand their attention, Clint and Blood had spent the remainder of the morning, with Brickhouse's permission, inspecting the *hacienda* and its defenses. The financier had accompanied them. At the conclusion, he had asked for their opinion of what they had seen. Clint had said he was satisfied with the arrangements, particularly the pump in the wine cellar as this would ensure a supply of drinking water in the event of an attack developing into a lengthy siege. When Blood had commented upon the difficulty of leaving the premises, should such a situation arise, Brickhouse replied that he had no fears on that account. He did not, however, elaborate upon the reason for his confidence.

By the time the tour was completed, the Texans and the financier found that most of the white men on the premises had gathered in the dining room for lunch. All through the meal, it had been obvious that Torreson was not in the best of moods. A comment from Earl Newton about how Claude Bigelow would have found it impossible to eat the tender steak if he had been present had provoked a biting remark from the New Yorker, and Blood's equally heated response.

"I know for sure, had it been me, I wouldn't have let 'em do it," Newton declared, and the other two men who had been in the dining room the previous night and during the display of gun handling given by the small Texan that morning muttered concurrence.

"There shouldn't've been any goddamned trouble in the first place!" Torreson objected, glancing about him in search of support.

"I didn't look for any," Clint asserted in a voice that was quiet and yet still sounded charged with deadly menace. "But I'll be damned if I'll back away from *anybody* who tries to push or ride me."

"Which *nobody* can blame you for, nor expect you to do, Rapido," Will Granger stated, remembering what he had witnessed on the range and realizing the time had come to show where his sympathies lay. "Those three got no more'n their needings and some'd say's they got even less."

"Which brings up something else, *Mr.* Torreson," the small Texan said coldly. "What he was saying down here, you'd told Bigelow about me."

"I'd said something about how you come here," the New Yorker admitted, albeit sounding a trifle defensive and uneasy.

"And about how *tough* I was?" Clint challenged, and the softly spoken words undoubtedly came into that category.

"From what I'd seen, you *are* tough!"

"I'm not gainsaying *that*. But anybody with *more* brains than a louse would have known saying it to a stupid, glory-hunting knothead like Bigelow—particularly where a feller my size is concerned—was sure to set him trying to prove different. And I reckon *you've* got *more* brains than a louse, *Mr.* Torreson."

"What's that mean?"

"Was I a suspicious man, I'd reckon you was counting on that hothead trying to take me when you told him."

"Why'd I do that?" Torreson asked, conscious that everybody present was listening and watching with great interest.

"To find out just how good I am—the *easy* way," Clint explained, lounging in what appeared to be a relaxed fashion on his chair. His cold gray eyes were fixed on the New Yorker's face as he continued speaking. "Which I reckon you *know* real good now."

Despite realizing that the small Texan had metaphorically thrown down a gauntlet, Torreson was disinclined to try to pick it up. Which placed him on the horns of a dilemma. He was aware that all the onlookers realized he was facing a deliberate challenge and appreciated the consequences should he decline to accept. Yet he was equally cognizant of the dangers involved if he offered defiance. He had seen how effectively Clint could handle a gun and conceded he was nowhere near as capable.

Like most criminals raised in the major cities of the East, he had invariably carried his gun in his pocket or waistband so as to allow it to be disposed of without leaving behind evidence that it had been on his person. And as the police with whom he had come up against were restricted in how effectively they could use their firearms by the equipment departmental regulations forced upon them, he had not found the need to acquire any ability in the matter of rapid drawing and shooting. Although he had taken to employing a shoulder holster since arriving in Mexico, he had not troubled to gain more than marginal skill in its use. Certainly he could not come close to competing with the small Texan on anything like equal terms.

"Have I told you what I've got planned for our entertainment tomorrow night, gentlemen?" Brickhouse asked soothingly, when the silence that had fallen after Clint delivered his challenge had endured for over half a minute. Sharing Torreson's views on the outcome of a confrontation, he had no desire for it to happen until a more propitious moment. Some of the men at the table had shown signs of supporting the New Yorker's point of view and he had no desire for a rift, with the possibility of losing more of the guard force, at that time. "I think you will find it *most* enjoy—"

"Boss!" Kenover yelled, dashing into the room before the financier could finish. "The wranglers've come back—without the hosses!"

"What happened?" Clint demanded, rising from his chair and speaking so quickly he anticipated a similar action and question from Torreson.

"They say a couple of *bandidos* jumped them—" Kenover started, glancing from the small Texan to the New Yorker then back. Having drawn the correct conclusions with regards to what he saw, he addressed Torreson.

*"Guevara's* men?" Torreson snarled, throwing a look filled with resentment at Clint for having so blatantly usurped his position.

"The wranglers allowed they were strangers," the messenger replied.

"Which don't mean *much*!" Torreson announced. "Even if we could trust those mother-something greasers to squeal on

their own kind, Guevara wouldn't send anybody they'd be likely
to know belonged to him. God damn it, I've been expecting
something like *this*. We should teach him a lesson!"

"How long ago did it happen?" Clint put in, seeing several
pairs of eyes—including those of Brickhouse—turned for guidance toward him.

"About half an hour after they'd set the *remuda* to grazing,"
Kenover answered, giving no indication that he was intimidated
by the scowl he received from the New Yorker. "They was left
hawg-tied and gagged so firm they've only just now got loose!"

"Or they—" Torreson interrupted.

"They'd been held firm enough, way their wrists 'n' ankles're
cut," Kenover asserted. "What do you want us to do—boss?"

"Go after the bastards!" Torreson commenced, once again
realizing the words had been directed to the small Texan in spite
of the honorific with which they ended.

"Are the rest of you in agreement with that?" Brickhouse
asked, but it was just as apparent to the New Yorker and everybody else that he too was speaking to Clint.

"I *would* be," the small Texan drawled, "except for one li'l
thing!"

"And what might that be, sir?" the financier wanted to know.

"Happen that Guevara had the *remuda* wide-looped, which I
don't reckon anybody would be likely to do it without his go-
ahead," Clint replied. "He'll've concluded we'll be so riled up
we'll figure on going after them. So he'll be ready and waiting—
and he'll have picked the place he's doing it at."

"That's a most reasonable assumption," Brickhouse said judi-
ciously, having seen many nods of agreement from around the
table.

"So *you* say we should just sit on our asses and let them get
away with it?" Torreson challenged, seeing his hold was slipping
over even those who had shown an inclination to support him
earlier in the conversation.

"Seeing that four of those horses belonged to Comanch' and

me, that's *not* what I'm saying," Clint corrected. "But neither do I see it'd be right good sense to go charging out of here like Colonel Teddy Roosevelt and the Rough Riders taking San Juan Hill. You can bet they'll have scouts out to watch for what we're doing."

"Knowing greasers from *way* back," Newton put in, "I can say for certain sure there will be."

"*Gracias, amigo,*" the small Texan drawled, nodding further gratitude for the confirmation of his summations. "So, happen there's some way Comanch', me, and a few others can get out without being seen, we'll take out their scouts and find out what's what. *Then* we can decide how to get the *remuda* back."

"Trouble's going to be getting out," Blood supplemented. "They'll be watching the gates and be able to see anybody trying to be sneaky and going over the walls. There's just *no* way of doing it by daylight, and I wouldn't even want to count on coming through unseen after dark, way the moon is."

"Could you get the horses back if there was a way out?" Brickhouse inquired.

"Only a fool would come right out and say yes to that, sir," Clint answered. "But I'll promise you one thing. Happen we can get out, we'll make a damned hard stab at doing it."

"Very well then," the financier said, after a moment during which he was clearly trying to reach a decision. "If there's *no* other way, I—"

Whatever Brickhouse was about to propose was brought to an end by the sound of running footsteps approaching across the entrance hall.

"Guevara and some of his bunch're coming!" announced Hank Wade, dashing into the room. "And they're bringing what looks like our *remuda* with them!"

"Good heavens!" Brickhouse exclaimed, which was the height of profanity for him. Despite realizing he could be acting in an impolitic manner, he could not prevent himself from continuing. "Now what do you make of *that,* Mr. Clint?"

"I wouldn't know," the small Texan confessed, aware that he was not the only person present to have noticed that the question was directed to him and not the previously acknowledged boss gun of the *Hacienda Naranja*. "But likely we'll find out when they get here." Swinging his gaze around the room, he went on in a more authoritative manner. "Comanch', find someplace where you can keep watch with that long shooting rifle of yours. I want the Brownings manned and everybody else rodded up, but out of sight. But keep your fingers off the triggers, unless it looks like trouble. Which I'm *not* expecting. *Move it!*"

As had happened earlier, Torreson was inclined to protest the usurping of his authority. Two things kept him silent. First, the rest of the men—including his former tentative adherents—were moving off to carry out the orders they had received. Second and of greater importance, he realized that to object would be tantamount to challenging Clint's authority. Having seen the other's smooth assumption of control and remembering the extraordinary speed with which the big Colt automatic pistol could be drawn and used, he had no wish to have it turned upon him. Which, he felt sure, would happen if he should have the temerity to state his point of view. Lacking the courage to take the stand his instincts demanded, he said and did nothing.

"Let's go and see what's doing!" the small Texan commanded, when all but himself, the financier, the New Yorker, and the two news bearers had taken their hurried departure. "And you'd *maybe* leave all the talking to Mr. Brickhouse and me, *Mr.* Torreson, seeing how we know Mexicans a heap better than *you.*"

"It would be *advisable,*" the financier confirmed, showing he was flattered by the compliment and leaving no doubt where he was now placing his reliance for support. "Come along, gentlemen."

Giving the scowling fugitive from New York no chance to reply, Clint and Brickhouse followed the two guards. Muttering under his breath, Torreson brought up the rear as they made

their way across the patio to the main entrance. On arrival, after
an interrogative glance at the small Texan—who looked around
to ensure his instructions had been completed and nodded when
satisfied—Brickhouse ordered the gates opened. While speaking, he realized that in similar circumstances, Torreson would
have given the command instead of allowing him to do so. It
was only a small matter, especially in such a potentially tense
situation, but it increased his belief that the *big* young Texan
would make a more satisfactory second in command than the
man who had claimed that position without consulting him
upon their arrival in Mexico.

If Clint was aware of the way in which his behavior was
gaining the approbation of his employer, he gave no sign of it.
Instead, he stood in silence and with his left hand gripping the
side of the leather jacket in what appeared to be a casual gesture
unless one knew of the big Colt it concealed. His whole attention was directed toward the entrance and the approaching
party that came into view when the gates were opened. All were
Mexicans, three riding ahead while the other four followed at a
slower pace with the *hacienda*'s *remuda* under their control.

"*Saludos, Don Alberto!*" greeted the man in the center of the
trio, his voice harsh and hoarse, as he brought his magnificent
white stallion to a stop in front of the financier's party.

"*Saludos, Señor* Guevara," Brickhouse replied, and continued in good Spanish. "To what do I owe the honor of this visit?"

Except for his mount and its costly, silver-decorated saddle
and bridle, there was little about Cristóbal Guevara to indicate
that he was the leader of the local *bandidos*. Bare-headed, big,
hard-looking and middle age, he had gray hair and a brutal face.
Despite being the well-educated son of a wealthy businessman,
he had learned early in life the benefits of posing as a defender of
the downtrodden poor. His manners were therefore uncouth, his
speech coarse, and he neither washed nor shaved to excess. A
worn old multihued shirt hung outside equally grubby and aged
trousers, while he wore only sandals on his filthy feet. His gun-

belt supported a plain Colt Civilian model Peacemaker in its holster on the right, and a fighting knife was sheathed at the left.

The man to Guevara's left was short, thick-set, evil-featured, and of indeterminate age. He obviously had a strong proportion of Indian blood, and he was just as poorly dressed as his superior and even dirtier. Although he had no handgun, a Winchester 1873 model rifle rested across his knees and a long machete dangled from his waist belt. He was *el Toro,* "the Bull," and *segundo* of the band.

At the right of the three, Che Orlando was a direct contrast to his companions. Guevara's favorite nephew, he was in his middle twenties. Tall, slender, handsome, he wore the *charro* attire of a wealthy *vaquero* and was superbly mounted. While similar to that of his uncle, his armament was far more costly in appearance. His expression and bearing suggested arrogance mixed with cruelty.

"Some of my boys found two men driving your *remuda, amigo,*" Guevara replied. "So, seeing we've got an agreement, they took them and I'm bringing them back."

"Did you get the men who had them?" Clint inquired.

"No," the *bandido* leader admitted, after running a speculative gaze over the small Texan. "Knowing the word I passed about Don Alberto and everything he owns, they got the hell out of it as soon as my boys came into sight."

"I'm grateful to you, *Señor* Guevara," Brickhouse declared. "Can I offer you drinks, or anything?"

"Not right now," the Mexican replied. "I thought I'd come over and explain myself, so nobody got the wrong idea. I've done it and I'll be going. See you tomorrow evening."

"Do you believe what he said?" the financier asked Clint, after the Mexicans had ridden away leaving the *remuda* just outside the gates.

"It *could* be the truth," the small Texan judged. "Or he might be showing you what'll happen if he doesn't get the extra money he's asking for."

"We ought to have shot all three of them while we'd the chance!" Torreson growled.

"It's lucky for you-all that you didn't try," Clint warned. "Comanch's watching and he knows what I wanted down here. He'd have blown your head off happen you'd tried anything so goddamned *loco* as doing that."

# 13
# I'VE ALWAYS *LOVED* TO FIGHT

"Isn't this The Battle at Bearcat Annie's?" Rita Ansell inquired, having walked over to point at the appropriate painting on the wall of the library.

"It is, my dear," Albert Brickhouse confirmed, gazing at the shapely brunette with added interest. "But I'm surprised that you recognized it."

"I couldn't fail to!" Rita declared in a tone that the financier recognized—although he was hardly able to believe it possible—as that of a fellow enthusiast. "But *this* is by far the best I've *ever* seen of it. And, my heavens, just look at all these others!"

"It seems you find my little collection of interest," Brickhouse remarked.

"I do, sir!" the brunette agreed.

"Perhaps Mr. Brickhouse will let you look around before you . . . go out?" Minnie Lassiter suggested.

"She won't be able to by the time I've finished with her!" Daisy Extall threatened, glowering at her opponent.

Friday and Saturday morning had passed uneventfully for the

two antagonists at the Premier Chicken Ranch. Obedient to the instructions they had received from the madam, they had kept out of the reception room and avoided coming into contact with one another elsewhere. Nor had they spoken during the journey by car to the *Hacienda Naranja.* They had been driven there, with Minnie sitting between them to ensure their good behavior, by Otis Garnell, and had arrived shortly before six o'clock in the evening.

On being admitted to the *hacienda,* the party had been greeted by Rapido Clint. He had told them that none of the guests had arrived, but Brickhouse was waiting to meet them in the library. From what they had seen on their way there, everything was ready for the *fiesta* that evening. Tables had been placed in a square on the edge of the patio, but there were chairs around the outsides only. In the center, the hard ground had been covered by sacks sewn together to make a single sheet and beneath which was a thick layer of straw. Feeling the surface give under their feet as they were walking across, none of them had needed to ask why so much trouble had been taken to produce this effect. It was a precaution taken to ensure that the fight was not ended prematurely by one or both the combatants falling on the unyielding stone slabs of the patio, thus sustaining injuries that would prevent them from continuing.

For her part, Minnie had been intrigued by the discovery that the small Texan appeared to have usurped Victor Torreson's position as the financier's second in command. Hoping to learn more about him, she had contacted the madam of the best brothel in Fort Worth on Thursday evening and requested information. The reply, which came late on Friday afternoon, had not entirely satisfied her curiosity. She had been told that little was known about Rapido Clint and Comanche Blood, other than that recently they had been mentioned as the perpetrators of several armed robberies in the vicinity. While a German girl had been raped and brutally beaten, due to the influence of her wealthy family and out of respect for her feelings, the local law

enforcement agencies had kept all reference to it out of the
newspapers. All the madam could say on the matter was that no
arrest had been made, nor could she find out who was suspected
as being responsible.

Although Minnie was only slightly better informed, she had
not ceased to consider Clint and Blood as potential recruits for
Hogan Turtle's organization. However, after escorting her party
to the library, the small Texan had left before she could offer to
apologize for her behavior during the latter part of his hectic
visit to the Premier Chicken Ranch. This, she had realized,
must be done as a prelude to becoming better acquainted with
him. Being more convinced than ever of his usefulness and capability, she was willing to shelve her pride and make the apology
in order to achieve her ends.

Brickhouse had greeted the madam warmly. On being introduced to Rita and Daisy, he had studied them with an anticipa-
tory and lascivious eagerness. After they had shaken hands, the
brunette had shown an interest in his collection of paintings and
the conversation was begun that ended with the redhead's
threatening comment.

For his part, the financier was in too jovial and expansive a
mood to be put out by Daisy's remark. In fact, he considered it
to be evidence of the continuing improvement in his current
state of affairs. It suggested there genuinely was no love lost
between herself and the brunette, which boded well for the fight
they were to have later.

The remainder of Friday had been without incident for Brickhouse, although beneficial in other ways. Three hardcases seeking employment had arrived shortly after Cristóbal Guevara
and his *bandidos* had taken their departure. Then another four
had put in an appearance during the evening.

Nor had the financier any complaints over the way in which
Saturday had progressed so far. After breakfast, Clint had established a moral ascendancy over the newcomers by thrashing the
biggest of them with an exhibition of a remarkably effective

barehanded fighting technique. Despite the disparity in their sizes, he had been left unmarked and unharmed. His antagonist had needed to be carried away in a battered and unconscious condition. Although Torreson had clearly been disappointed, the rest of the old hands were delighted by the result and accepted the *big* young Texan unreservedly as their leader. Furthermore, when the fugitive from New York had attempted to follow his usual procedure by taking his spite out on Wildersleeve, Clint had intervened and Torreson had once again been compelled to back down, losing still more face.

Finally, under the valet's supervision, there had been no snags in the domestic arrangements. And from all appearances, not only were the combatants as shapely as promised by the madam, it was obvious they disliked one another intensely.

All in all, Brickhouse was confident that the *fiesta* would prove to be a success and produce the desired results.

"Wildersleeve will show you to your rooms, ladies," the financier announced, returning to the desk and pressing the bell button on it. "I presume you will be staying the night, Miss Lassiter?"

"I think it will be necessary," the madam admitted. "Neither of the ladies will be up to traveling when it is over."

"Then I hope you will be my guest at the head table?" Brickhouse offered.

"I'll be honored, sir," Minnie replied, her tone implying she expected no other treatment. "Come, ladies."

"Might I stay and look at the rest of these wonderful pictures first, please?" Rita requested eagerly.

"Of course you may," Brickhouse assented without a moment's hesitation, the question having been directed more to him than the madam. "If that's all right with you, of course, Miss Lassiter?"

"I've no objections," Minnie declared. Despite being disinclined to leave the brunette and the financier together in case he should disclose the exact sum he was paying for the fight, she

realized that a refusal in the face of his obvious willingness
might provoke comments. "But I feel, if you're to put on the
kind of performance Mr. Brickhouse expects from you, it would
be advisable for you to rest and be refreshed when the time
comes."

"It won't take long," the financier promised. "Ah, Wildersleeve. Show these two ladies to their rooms, then come back for
Miss Ansell."

"Yes, sir," the valet assented, having just entered in response
to the bell's summons. He looked at Rita for a moment. "Come
this way, please, ladies."

"I sense you are an enthusiast on this subject, like myself,"
Brickhouse remarked, after the two women had been escorted
from the library, waving a hand toward the paintings and making no attempt to conceal his desire to hear an affirmative answer.

"I am sir, I really *am!*" Rita confirmed. "I've always *loved* to
fight!" After pausing for a couple of seconds and eyeing the
financier in a seductive fashion, she went on. "And, after I've
been in a fight, I'm really ready to start making *love.*"

"I *see,* my dear!" Brickhouse breathed, running the tip of his
tongue over his thick lips as he contemplated some of the pos-
sibilities implied by the brunette's comment. "How deeply are
you committed to Miss Lassiter?"

"Not at all, sir," Rita stated. "I only started at her place on
Thursday morning and, because of the trouble with that fat
cow, I haven't been allowed to turn a single trick. So I don't owe
her a thing."

*"Good!"* Brickhouse said amiably, deciding against inquiring
how much the madam was paying the combatants. He suspected the sum would be lower than the amount Minnie was
receiving, but he refrained from mentioning this. It would prevent the madam from raising objections should the offer he was
going to make to Rita be accepted. "Then you would be willing
to consider taking another . . . position?

"Where and what kind of a 'position'?"

"Here, as my female champion."

*"Champion?"* Rita repeated. "Do you mean—"

"You will live here and take on any women challengers who are brought to meet you," Brickhouse affirmed. He had detected a note in the brunette's voice that indicated this was exactly the kind of offer she was hoping for. Seeing a way of ensuring she gave of her best against the redhead, he finished, "Providing you *win* tonight, of course."

"I'm going to do my damnedest to win!" Rita declared, glancing at the dainty handbag she was holding. Thinking of one of the items it contained and the reason for which she had contrived to be brought to the *Hacienda Naranja,* she went on in a grimly determined fashion that—although he was under a misapprehension about its meaning—delighted the financier. "And *you* can count on *that!*"

Despite having achieved her purpose, so far as making the acquaintance and arousing the interest of Albert Brickhouse, Rita Ansell needed to call upon all her resolve before she could start walking across the padded surface of the patio toward the table at which the main guests were seated. For all the preparations she had made, she knew that defeating Daisy Extall would be anything but a snap. However, thoughts of the consequences of being defeated were not the cause of her qualms. Studying the lust-filled faces of most of the men who were spectators, she felt close to being nauseated by what she read from their expressions.

To take her mind off the uneasiness she was experiencing (knowing it could have a detrimental effect upon her chances of winning), the brunette thought of the competent way in which Minnie Lassiter had arranged for the fight to take place.

After calling the combatants to her room shortly before the event was due to commence, the madam had ordered them to strip off all their clothes. When this had been done, she had searched them to make sure they had no weapons of any kind concealed on their persons or in their hair. Satisfied on this point, she had handed each a tiny black G-string such as was employed as a final item of attire by striptease artists in burlesque theaters. Giving them no time to comment, she had said they were not to commence the fight clad solely in the minute garments. She explained what was wanted of them, indicating two piles of clothing on her bed and asking them to dress.

The disputed pair of black silk stockings were among the garments allocated to Daisy, and there was another pair for Rita. Along with a garter belt, a suitable brassiere and panties, each had been given a stylish, sleeveless satin evening gown of extreme décolleté to complete her ensemble. Showing an interest in their future, although she knew only one would be remaining in her employment after the fight—but being unaware of the brunette's offer from Brickhouse—Minnie had insisted they remove all their jewelry. As a further precaution against the creation of disfiguring scars, she had made each contender put on short black leather gloves. These were fastened around the wrists to prevent their removal, thus avoiding the damage that could ensure if fingernails were brought into use.

When she was almost at the head table, Rita put aside her contemplations. Listening to the rumble of comments that were going on all around her, she realized that everybody in the patio had either been informed of or suspected what was going to happen. Sucking in a deep breath, she gave all her attention to considering how she could ensure she qualified for the position that had been offered to her. Only by doing so could she achieve the purpose for which she was willing to undergo such humiliation, hardship, and danger.

# 14

# THE BEST FIGHT I'VE
# *EVER* SEEN

Watching Rita Ansell and Daisy Extall kicking off their shoes prior to approaching across the patio, Minnie Lassiter wondered how well they would acquit themselves. She felt sure there was little danger of them doing so poorly that she would be required to refund the money she had received from Albert Brickhouse.

Remembering how much difficulty she had experienced in beating the redhead—despite the advantages of her use of *savate* and having had the hard-packed points of her ballet slippers to add force to her kicking—on the occasion at the Premier Chicken Ranch when they had fought, the madam had no doubts that Daisy would fight well. Furthermore, the search for weapons earlier that evening had established that the brunette was remarkably fit for a girl following the occupation of prostitute.

As the pair had not lost any of their animosity toward one another since their abortive conflict on Thursday, Minnie was satisfied they could be counted upon to give of their best. Nor did she consider it a matter for concern that they were carrying out her instructions by walking side by side toward where she was sitting, instead of starting to fight as soon as they left the main building. It was merely a sign that they were still respectful of her authority. Their removal of their shoes indicated each had appreciated how she would be able to move more freely on the yielding surface in her bare feet. It was further evidence of a mutual determination to emerge victorious.

Running a quick gaze around the patio, the madam told herself—not for the first time—that she could find no fault with the financier's arrangements and hospitality. However, nothing had occurred to cause her to revise her first impression that the quality of the guests was far from worthy of the amount of effort and money expended to entertain them. Although she did not include the fee offered to Rita and Daisy, whose participation she considered was as much to satisfy Brickhouse's predilection for the erotic pleasure of watching women fighting as for the enjoyment of the guests, the cost of the *fiesta* would still be considerable. In addition to the lavish feast that had just ended, there was the traditional Mexican band, flamenco dancers, and sufficient female company available to keep the guests occupied while awaiting the main event of the evening.

At the tables to the right and left of the patio sat a mixture of minor local officials, *bandidos,* and white men Minnie knew to be hardcases and criminals. Nor, with two exceptions, did she consider the guests who sat on either side of her to be much of an improvement socially. Apart from her host, Rapido Clint, Comanche Blood, and Victor Torreson, all were Mexicans. They were Cristóbal Guevara, his segundo, *el Toro,* and nephew, Che Orlando, the mayor, chief of police, a doctor, a banker, and two prominent businessmen from Juarez.

Although the madam had not yet found an opportunity to talk privately with the small Texan, she noticed that since sitting down he and his dark companion drank more sparingly than anybody else except herself and Brickhouse. She knew that, unless they had been requested to remain sober, no other reason except their personal preference was causing the two young men to display such abstinence. There had been—in fact, still was—food and drink in plenty for all who wished to indulge. It was being served, under the far from approving supervision of Wildersleeve and the *Hacienda Naranja*'s regular household staff, by the numerous attractive Mexican and Indian girls who had been hired from brothels in the surrounding district for the occasion.

Aware of what Brickhouse was hoping to achieve with the *fiesta,* Minnie considered it was much to the credit of the two Texans if they were carrying out his instructions by remaining sober. On the other hand, should they be refraining from drinking to excess of their own accord, it was an even greater point in their favor. No matter which it was, she had no doubt Hogan Turtle could make good use of men with such strength of will.

Realizing that the girls had arrived in front of the head table and halted, the madam put aside her thoughts of how she could persuade Clint and Blood to become members of Turtle's organization.

"These are the two young ladies I've been telling you about, Mr. Brickhouse, gentlemen!" Minnie announced, coming to her feet and causing an expectant silence to fall around the patio. "It seems that—"

Although she had done all she had been told by the madam up to that point, Daisy did not wait for the introductions to be completed. Instead, swinging her right arm sideways, she propelled her clenched fist so it struck Rita in the left breast. Caught unawares, the brunette gave a squeal of pain and staggered back a few steps. Delighted by the knowledge that there was no further need to exercise self-restraint, the redhead turned to continue the attack.

As in the fight that Minnie had ended in the reception room at the Premier Chicken Ranch, Rita acted swiftly and capably to defend herself. After leaping aside at the last moment before Daisy reached her, she swung around. Before the redhead could

turn, the straps of her blue satin evening gown were jerked
down over her shoulders. Having achieved this, the brunette
pulled her in a circle and started to slap her face with each hand
in succession. Four times the flat palms landed on Daisy's
cheeks. Screeching as her head was rocked from side to side by
the impacts, she gave a jerk that snapped the strap and liberated
her left hand. Having done so, she threw a punch. The knuckles
met Rita's nose, jolting her head to the rear and causing her to
withdraw involuntarily.

Relieved of the pressure, the redhead extracted her other arm.
Without waiting to return the unbroken strap to its original
position, she lunged forward. Paying just as little attention to
the tears caused by the punch on the nose, the brunette sprang
to meet her. As they clashed together, each seized the other's
hair with both hands. Urged onward by cheers from almost all
of the spectators around the patio, they struggled in that fashion
for a few seconds in an instinctive attempt to wrestle one another to the ground. Then, making the most of her slight weight
advantage, Daisy managed to tilt Rita backward. Hooking her
right leg behind the brunette's left, the redhead destroyed her
equilibrium. However, as she was going down, Rita clung to
Daisy and twisted aside as the other was compelled to go down
with her.

Although their landing jolted the girls apart, they stayed that
way only long enough to get to their knees. Without attempting
to rise, they got to grips again. Slapping, punching, then grabbing hair, they struggled back to their feet. Having done so, it
seemed at first that they would remain locked together in that
fashion. Suddenly, as they surged together, Daisy brought up
her left knee. Caught in the body, Rita gave a cry and moved
back, trying to break loose. Grinning in triumph, the redhead
opened her hands and put them to work repaying the slaps she
had received earlier. Gasping and driven backward by the vigorous assault, Rita brought it to an end by jabbing her left fist
hard into Daisy's stomach. As the buxom girl doubled up, her

hair was grasped by the brunette's right hand and the left continued to strike at her head and shoulders. Thrusting herself forward, her attempt to deliver a butt was thwarted. Instead, she wrapped her arms around her assailant's thighs and they once more went to the floor.

This time the combatants neither separated nor came to their knees. Rolling over and over, they alternated among pulling hair, swinging blows, and grappling with each other. Finding her green gown being dragged upward over her head while she was momentarily on top of Daisy, threatening to trap her as well as prevent her from seeing what was happening, Rita part wriggled and part tore herself free of it. Appreciative yells arose on all sides as she emerged, clad only in her underclothing and with her stockings already laddered, to be rolled over and straddled by the redhead. The shouts increased in volume very shortly. Wanting to escape from beneath Daisy, who was using her hair to bang her head on the ground, the brunette sank her fingers into the other's big bosom. Jerking back to rid herself of the painful pressure, Daisy left her brassiere in Rita's grasp. However, although a surging heave rid herself of the redhead's weight, the brunette's own brassiere was ripped away in retaliation to leave them both bare to the waist.

The combatants were oblivious to their breasts being exposed to the lascivious stares of the men at the tables. Having inadvertently carried out the madam's instructions to make sure they tore off some of each other's clothing while fighting, the girls continued to struggle with an equal violence and determination. Soon both were bleeding from the nostrils and a couple of places where bites had been inflicted. Their skin showed reddening caused by slaps, clutching fingers, or being rubbed against the harsh texture of the sacking upon which they were recklessly thrashing. Regaining their feet, they surged back and forward across the open space. They traded punches and slaps to the head, breasts, or stomach with wild abandon, kicked or used their knees just as indiscriminately. Then they wrestled with hands interlocked in a trial of pure primeval strength, until inadvertently tripped and sent down once more.

The cycle of rising and going down was repeated three more times. During the unrelenting battle, Daisy's gown had been ripped off and the stockings that had been the cause of the original conflict were left kneeless and scarred by runs. Minnie's wisdom in supplying the G-strings was demonstrated when the elastic in the redhead's panties broke and they slid down to be kicked off as a dangerous encumbrance. Shortly after, while wriggling from between Daisy's thighs, Rita was parted from her nether garments as they were grabbed in an attempt to prevent her from escaping.

As with the loss of the brassieres, the state of near nudity to which the girls were reduced caused much vocal approbation among the male onlookers. It did nothing, however, to dampen the ardor with which they went on fighting. However, the pace and the suffering each was inflicting began to have effect. Both were glistening with perspiration to such an extent that it was diluting the blood they were shedding, and their hair looked like tangled, soddened mops. No longer did either squeal, or cry out; they had no breath to spare and were having difficulty, as their heaving bosoms showed, in even keeping their tormented lungs replenished.

Feeling on the verge of collapsing with exhaustion, only the thought of what she was hoping to achieve as a result of victory gave Rita the fortitude to keep going. On one occasion, while being dragged across the patio by the hair after being thrown down hard, she had almost passed out. There had been other times, particularly when her large breasts were being crushed and punched by Daisy and circumstances temporarily prevented her from retaliation, when she had thought she was finished. On each occasion, the remembrance of why she had come to the *Hacienda Naranja* caused her to make the determined effort needed to escape and inflict a similar punishment upon the redhead's even larger and equally vulnerable bosom.

Daisy lacked any such deeply compelling inducement. What was more, she was older and less fit than the brunette. Despite having had periods when she dominated the action, each time she had felt sure victory was—almost literally once or twice—in her grasp, Rita had contrived to turn the tables and repay her treatment with interest. The moments of ascendancy had declined as the younger girl steadfastly refused to be beaten, until the redhead was finding it increasingly difficult to hold her own. She was, in fact, receiving the kind of beating she had frequently dealt to fellow workers who had aroused her bad temper.

At last the strain of the punishment being inflicted upon her became too much for Daisy to endure.

Letting out a moan of fright, the redhead took advantage of a punch to her breast that sent her close to her opponent and tried to flee. As she turned and began to stumble away on legs that could barely support her weight, the brunette tackled her around the waist and brought her to the ground. In spite of the thick layer of straw beneath the sacking, the impact jolted what little breath remained from her bruised and battered body. She was still conscious, but in no condition to resist when she felt herself being rolled on to her back.

Advancing on spread-apart knees until straddling the plump torso and sitting on the weakly moving stomach, Rita showed Daisy no mercy. Even if she had been inclined to do so, after all she had suffered at the other's hands, she dared not offer an opportunity for recovery. She was too close to collapse herself to take such a chance. Bracing herself by sinking the fingers and thumb of her right hand into the redhead's left breast, provoking a feeble and instinctive writhing from the body between her thighs, she used the other fist to deliver two punches and two backhand blows to Daisy's chin. Only the first to land was required to render the redhead completely unconscious, but it was the brunette's physical condition that prevented more from being delivered. Knowing she was almost spent when she could not make the fifth blow, her feeling of alarm was dissipated by a realization that there was no longer any movement from Daisy.

Relief welled through Rita at the appreciation that the fight was at long last over and she had won. As she was beginning to rise, she remembered what had caused the conflict. Pure instinct rather than any conscious guidance on her part caused her to shuffle slowly around on her skinned and sore knees. Although moving grew increasingly difficult by the second, oblivious to the tumultuous reception being accorded to her by the spectators, she dragged the tattered remnants of the black silk stockings from Daisy's legs.

Completing the task was all the brunette could manage. Blackness welled over her and she flopped backward across her defeated opponent.

"By gad, Miss Lassiter!" Brickhouse gasped, turning his sweat-sodden face toward the madam and speaking breathlessly. "If only I'd thought to hire a moving picture camera! They were worth every red cent I paid for them! That was the best fight I've *ever* seen!"

"I'm pleased you approve," Minnie replied, and continued without saying that she was in agreement with the financier's last sentence. "Now I'll trouble you to have the doctor attend to the ladies and to make your—*guests*—remain on the outside of the tables until after they've been removed."

"Stay where you are, please, all of you!" the financier shouted in Spanish, standing and raising his far from inconsiderable voice so that it carried around the patio and silenced the vociferous approbation being expressed by the spectators. "Don't anybody come beyond the tables until the ladies have been taken indoors."

Although the general tendency was to respect the wishes of their host, particularly as Wildersleeve set the Mexican girls—who had been so enthralled by the fight that they had neglected their duties—to work delivering drinks, a burly *bandido* at the far end of the right side table showed he had no such intention.

A cousin of *el Toro* and noted for his truculence, he had taken sufficient drink to forget the orders given by Guevara regarding good behavior during the *fiesta*. Swaying as he moved, but looking meaner than a bull elk bugling at rivals during the rutting season, he slouched from his place and on to the patio.

Even before Brickhouse could look in his direction, much less speak, Rapido Clint was on his feet. Although he was carrying his Colt Government model .45 automatic pistol in its shoulder holster and had an even more potent weapon just as readily available, he made no attempt to arm himself. Instead, placing his left hand on the table, he vaulted across it. Striding forward swiftly, causing the rumble of talk that had risen at the sight of the *bandido*'s behavior to die away, he went past the recumbent and almost naked girls to halt between them and the approaching man.

As on numerous other occasions in the past, the deceptive nature of Clint's physical appearance proved advantageous.

Staring at the diminutive figure that was confronting him as if hardly able to believe it was there, the big *bandido* muttered a profanity and swung his right arm around in a manner similar to that he would have used when brushing away a bothersome insect. Instantly Clint demonstrated how well he could cope with such a situation. Moving clear, he caught his would-be assailant's wrist in both hands and twisted around so the limb was resting across his left shoulder. Then, sinking to his right knee, he applied a leverage that catapulted the *bandido* over him.

Known as a "flying mare," among other names, there were two ways in which such a throw could be executed.

By allowing the recipient's trapped arm to be bent, the result was comparatively innocuous. Aware of the risks involved when contending against such a large and potentially dangerous antagonist, the small Texan adopted the second method.

On gripping the wrist, moving so swiftly that the *bandido* had no chance to resist, Clint turned it so the palm of the hand was

upward. By doing so, he prevented the elbow from being able to
perform its natural function of bending. Not only did this have
the effect of increasing the impact with which the recipient
landed on his back, it also dislocated his shoulder. For all that,
snarling further pain-filled and gasping profanities, the *bandido*
thrust himself into a sitting position. His left hand reached for
the revolver tucked into the sash around his waist.

The attempt at reprisal was to no avail.

After stepping to one side, the *bandido*'s attacker sent a kick
to his chin with such force he was not only rendered unconscious, his jaw was broken.

Angry comments rumbled from among the other *bandidos* on
the side tables. Although they were amazed by what had happened, they began to stand up with the intention of avenging
their stricken companion. What was more, showing just as
strenuous a disapproval, Orlando and *el Toro* also started to
rise.

Rapido Clint's foresight ended the threat of disruption to the
peaceful nature of the *fiesta*.

When the small Texan had come to his feet, his dark companion had not needed to be told what he intended to do. However,
Blood had no intention of intervening with bare hands. Instead,
he made ready to give support by taking advantage of a safety
measure Clint had caused to be carried out.

Suspecting there might be trouble, particularly in view of the
lavish way in which their employer was intending to supply
drinks to the guests, the small Texan had arranged for two sets
of hooks to be fitted under the table at the places where he and
Blood would be sitting.

Each set held a fully loaded Winchester 1897 model trench
gun.

Liberating his weapon as his *amigo* was advancing to con-
front the burly *bandido*, Blood rose. He bounded onto the table
and worked the cocking slide with a deft flick of his left wrist,

then he fired the shell he had loaded and sent its charge into the air.

"She's filled with nine buckshot, *señores!*" the dark Texan warned in the kind of Spanish spoken along the border between the United States and Mexico. While delivering the warning, he operated the mechanism to remove the empty case and feed another live shell into the chamber of the trench gun. Swinging its barrel in an arc that encompassed both sides of the patio and ended with the muzzle pointing at Orlando, he continued, "So *everybody* just stay put and enjoy the drinks."

Although as angry as any of his men over the way in which *el Toro*'s cousin had been treated, justified though the treatment undoubtedly was, Guevara was sufficiently sober to appreciate the full ramifications of the situation. Not only had he underestimated how many *gringo* hardcases were available, causing his party to lack numerical superiority, but there was another point to be taken into consideration. It would be impolitic to antagonize the local dignitaries who were present, not all of whom were under an obligation to him, by allowing the festivities to be brought to an untimely end as a result of trouble between the members of his band and the employees of their host. Furthermore, after having rendered Sanchez unconscious, the small—yet somehow big-looking—Texan had drawn a Colt automatic with impressive speed and was gazing at him in a way that suggested he would be its first target if hostilities commenced. He did not doubt that the skill displayed in producing the weapon would be backed by sufficient accuracy to put his life in jeopardy.

There was, the leader of the *bandidos* conceded grudgingly to himself, only one course open to him under the circumstances.

"Sit down and behave, all of you!" Guevara thundered, lurching erect and glaring about him, but making sure he kept his empty hands prominently displayed. "We're guests here, so do as Don Alberto's man told you!"

* * *

Forcing herself to accept the pain that moving produced, despite the ministrations she had received earlier from the doctor, Rita Ansell slowly eased herself into a sitting position. After shoving off the sheet that was covering her naked, bruised, but—as she had been bathed by two of the Mexican girls on being carried upstairs—clean body, she swung out her legs to lower her feet to the floor. The room's light was on. Picking up the wristwatch she had left on the dressing table when she had been summoned by Minnie Lassiter to make ready for the fight, she squinted at its face through her swollen and discolored right eye. The left was so puffed up that she could not see through it at all.

The examination informed the brunette that, although she could still hear music and other sounds of festivity from the patio, three hours had elapsed since she had fallen in a faint induced by exhaustion to lay supine on the unconscious body of Daisy Extall. While she had been given all the care and attention possible under the circumstances, she had only just thrown off the effects of her sufferings sufficiently to be able to take notice of her surroundings. In fact, even with the remembrance that she had won the fight and the knowledge of what the victory meant to help her, it was a tribute to her fortitude and strength of will that she was able to drag herself into consciousness.

The first movements Rita had made caused her to feel in torment, but she refused to yield to the impulse to lie down again. She was goaded by the belief that, as she was in a comatose state which was neither asleep nor awake, somebody had been at her bedside. When she had opened her good eye, the door was closing. While she had not seen who was leaving, she thought it was Albert Brickhouse and he had paid the visit to offer her the "position" they had discussed in the library. Feeling sure he would return, or come later if it had been somebody else, she wanted to make sure everything was ready for receiving him.

After returning the watch to the dressing table, the brunette took her handbag from the drawer in which she had placed it. Opening it and delving inside, her fingers scrabbled in an increasingly desperate attempt to locate what they were seeking. Gasping in anxiety, she upturned the bag and spilled its contents on the bed. Her restricted vision notwithstanding, she discovered that everything was there except the most important article of all. Filled with alarm, as she had checked it was there before leaving for the fight, she wondered who had removed the small vial of poison that she had intended to administer to the financier when he came to congratulate her on her victory.

# 15

# GUEVARA WANTS CLINT AND BLOOD

"*Hombre*, the only reason you're losing so heavy is you're a lousy card player. Fact being, I'll bet you're so stupid you couldn't even set fire to a cube of sugar."

Hearing Comanche Blood delivering the comment in a mocking voice, as he was walking down the stairs from the upper floor of the *Hacienda Naranja*'s main building, Rapido Clint made his way across the entrance hall to the open double doors of the dining room.

What the small Texan had already seen as he was commencing his descent made him put from his mind something he had just discovered. He had been sent by Albert Brickhouse to ascertain whether Rita Ansell was sufficiently recovered from her exertions to join the guests of honor at the head table and receive their congratulations. Although as far as he could tell, she had either been asleep or still unconscious, he had made a discovery that puzzled and disturbed him.

Confident he could leave his curiosity where the brunette was concerned until a more propitious moment, Clint gave all his attention to what was happening in the dining room. However, having approached quickly and quietly, he did not enter. Instead, as everybody present was watching Blood and the person to whom the derogatory words were directed, he halted just outside the doors to await the developments his instincts warned him would shortly be forthcoming.

After the unconscious fighters and the *bandido* felled by the small Texan had been removed, a poker game had started in the dining room despite there being music and female company available on the patio. The original players, Blood, Hank Wade, Earl Newton, Will Granger, and one of the newly arrived hardcases, had been augmented by Che Orlando and *el Toro,* neither of whom had found the company at the head table to their taste.

Knowing his *amigo*'s ability as a poker player, Clint was not surprised to see that he was winning a good sum of money. Nor, as he had formed a shrewd assessment of Orlando's character and lack of skill as a gambler, did he consider it in the least out of the ordinary that the young Mexican would be one of the heavy losers. In fact, he regarded Orlando's chances of winning against such opposition to be on a par with that of a rat dropped into a barrel with a bull terrier. What was more, taking into account the way in which Blood's insulting words had been framed, he guessed what might be coming. He also felt that his undetected presence could prove advantageous should his assumptions prove correct, which was why he did not enter the dining room or go to report the result of his mission to the financier.

"What do you mean?" Orlando demanded angrily, speaking fluent English with a slight Hispanic accent.

"Just what I said," Blood answered, placing the thin black cheroot he was smoking on the ashtray by his side and waving the hand he had been using in the direction of the tray upon which coffee had been brought for the players. "I'll bet you-all don't have sense enough to set fire to one of those sugar cubes."

"How much will you bet?" Orlando challenged, his face tak-

ing on a crafty expression as he thought of how easily sugar
would burn when poured on to a fire.

"Well, now—" Blood began, showing the kind of nervous
hesitancy that a more observant person might have remembered
had been simulated by him on the occasion during the game
when he had been dealt a small straight flush pat hand.*

"What's a matter, *gringo*?" Orlando mocked. "Do you only
make bets with your mouth?"

"I wouldn't say *that*!" Blood replied, showing what appeared
to be annoyance.

"Then put up or shut up!" Orlando stated in a hostile fashion.

"All right, happen that's how *you-all* want it," the Texan
acceded, seemingly reluctant. "All I've got here against your
pile and that fancy-handled six-gun you're toting."

"You're on!" the young *bandido* accepted, concluding that—
even with the price of his favorite revolver included—there was
more money in front of his opponent than he had in his possession.

Exchanging brief knowing looks and winks, the longer serving of the hardcases watched a repetition of the way in which
their employer had conducted the wager with each of them in
turn on their arrival to work for him. Deducing that Blood had
discovered the secret, all of them wanted to see if they could
detect how it was performed. Despite showing signs of suspecting something was amiss, *el Toro* made no attempt to dissuade his young companion. Instead, he suggested similar precautions to those taken by all the previous victims including
Clint two nights earlier.

"All right!" the younger *bandido* snarled, showing alarm and

---

* For the benefit of new readers: a straight flush—that is, two, three, four,
five, six of the same suit—is dealt "pat" when the cards are delivered
consecutively instead of some needing to be obtained by drawing from the
deck. An explanation of the various types of poker hands and their respective values is given in *Two Miles to the Border*. *J.T.E.*

consternation when his attempt to set the sugar cube alight produced only a brown and sticky mess. "Let's see *you* make the goddamned thing burn!"

Even before Blood could make the suggestion, *el Toro* demanded that Orlando's matches be used. Assenting, Blood asked for one to be lighted. Taking advantage of the distraction caused by this being done, he swiftly dipped the sticky side of the cube so a small portion of the ash from the tray adhered to it. Clint had explained what would happen while they were alone on Friday. He had refrained from exposing the trick in order to gain Brickhouse's good offices. Being a vegetable carbon, the ash acted as a catalyst and, when the lighted match was applied, the cube burst into flame.

"Is that *good* enough?" the Texan asked, dropping the burning cube into the ashtray and reaching down to wipe his fingers on the front of his trousers.

"It's a trick, god damn it!" Orlando shouted furiously, rising with such violence that he sent his chair skidding away behind him. "Well, here's my *gun!*"

While spitting out the second sentence, the young *bandido* grabbed swiftly for the holstered revolver. However, as his hand closed about the ornate butt, it was obvious that he was not intending to pass the weapon over in payment of the wager he had lost. His thumb curled over and drew back the hammer. What was more, as soon as the Colt rose far enough to allow access, his forefinger entered the guard to depress the trigger.

Startled exclamations burst from the hardcases, and they all rose hurriedly with the intention of escaping from the line of fire. Also standing up with alacrity, *el Toro* started to pull his *machete* from its sheath.

Blood made no attempt to leave his chair.

Remaining seated, the dark Texan plucked the knife—the hilt of which he had already grasped under the pretense of wiping his hand—away from its sheath. Coming up and into view, it was flung in a single blur of motion across the table.

Glinting briefly in the electric light as it sped through the air, the spear-pointed blade of the knife sank into Orlando's left shoulder at a most inauspicious moment. So swiftly had everything happened that the five-and-a-half-inch "Artillery model" barrel of his Peacemaker had not quite cleared the lip of the holster when he was struck. Which proved most unfortunate for him. Shock and pain caused him to let go of the weapon. This in turn permitted the hammer to start moving before the liberated trigger could advance sufficiently to prevent its operation. There was the crash of a shot, and he screamed even louder as the .45-caliber bullet tore at an angle through his right thigh.*

Giving vent to a bellow of rage, which came close to duplicating the sound of his namesake when provoked, *el Toro* raised the *machete* and sprang toward the now-unarmed man who had caused his leader's nephew to be injured.

To all appearances, Comanche Blood had committed a grievous error in tactics.

For all that, the Texan was far from as reckless as he seemed. Having seen his *amigo* coming down the stairs and waiting at the doors, Blood had known help was at hand. Nor did the small Texan fail to justify his companion's confidence.

Drawing the big Colt Government model automatic pistol from his shoulder holster, Clint acted in the only way possible under the circumstances. Taking the brief time required to elevate the weapon to shoulder height and at arms' length in both hands, he aligned the sights. Firing, he sent the heavy-caliber bullet into the *bandido's* head.

Struck almost anywhere else, *el Toro* could have lived sufficiently long to carry out his intention of sinking the razor-sharp blade of the *machete* into Blood's skull. As it was, the hardcase

---

* For the benefit of new readers: Another example of how dangerous it could be to cock the hammer and draw back the trigger of a single-action revolver before its barrel had cleared the holster and was pointing away from the user is given in *The Fast Gun. J.T.E.*

was killed instantaneously, and his weapon flopped downward harmlessly. He was spun in a half circle, then measured his length on the floor.

"*Gracias,* Rapido!" Blood drawled, glancing gratefully at his savior.

"*Es nada, amigo,*" the small Texan replied, walking forward with the Colt in his right hand. "Only I don't reckon Cristóbal Guevara will see it *that* way when he finds out what we've had to do."

"Throw down your guns and get your hands high, you two sons of bitches!" Victor Torreson commanded, bringing a Colt Army 1917 model revolver from behind his back as he stepped into the entrance hall from the library of the *Hacienda Naranja*'s main building. He lined its barrel in the general direction of Rapido Clint and Comanche Blood. "And don't anybody else try to bill in if you value your hides!"

"Good heavens, man!" Albert Brickhouse gasped, moving hurriedly away from the two young Texans. "Whatever is possessing you?"

"Guevara wants Clint and Blood," the fugitive from New York replied, as the man who had received the beating from the small Texan moved forward, also drawing a revolver, and halted alongside him. "That was him on the Maw Bell just now.* He says he's got no quarrel with the rest of us and, if we send them out, he'll take his men away and leave us be."

As Clint had intimated, on Cristóbal Guevara's arrival in the dining room with the financier and other guests to investigate the cause of the disturbance, he had been far from enamored with the sight that greeted him. Nor had his temper been improved when the doctor had informed him that, even if Che

---

* "Ma Bell": Colloquialism for a telephone, derived from the name of its inventor, Scottish-born, American physicist Alexander Graham Bell (1847–1922). J.T.E.

Orlando survived the injury, there was no chance of saving the shattered limb and amputation would be necessary. For all that, faced with the practically unanimous hostility of the white hardcases and presented with indisputable evidence that his nephew and *segundo* had been the aggressors, he had managed to restrain his all-too-obvious anger. Warning his men against any attempt to avenge the stricken pair, he had told them to take *el Toro*'s body to their headquarters for burial and had left to accompany his nephew to the hospital in Juarez.

Despite Torreson's gloomy predictions, the night had passed without incident. However, before noon that day, every one of the Mexicans who had been on the premises had taken his departure. They had gone unannounced, in twos and small groups, leaving by alternate gates to avoid arousing the suspicions of the doubled guards, until none remained to be questioned about the reason for the mass exodus. There had been some comment when their desertion was discovered, but it did not go beyond complaints about the lack of amenities likely to be caused by their desertion. These had not eventuated. With the help of Rita Ansell—who had offered her services despite it being apparent she was still feeling the effects of her previous evening's exertions—and men assigned to the duty by Clint, Wildersleeve had produced a lunch as good as the meals to which the majority of the hardcases had become accustomed.

On being informed that the brunette had accepted Brickhouse's invitation to remain at the *Hacienda Naranja,* Minnie Lassiter had been annoyed. When she received a hint from the financier that her embezzlement in the matter of the payment for the two combatants would be exposed, however, she had yielded to the inevitable. While displeased by the loss of Rita, whom she had hoped to employ in a similar capacity to that which she suspected was intended by Brickhouse, she took consolation from the knowledge that the visit had otherwise been most fruitful.

Not only had the madam made a substantial financial profit

from the money received for supplying the fighters plus her unofficial levy out of the well-subscribed collection she had taken on their behalf the previous night, but she had made her peace with Rapido Clint. Taking an opportunity to speak in private with him, when he had thanked her for giving moral support against Guevara, she had started by apologizing for her behavior during their first meeting. Accepting, he had promised to give consideration to her proposal that he and Comanche Blood should join Hogan Turtle's organization when their period of employment with Brickhouse was terminated.

Torreson's warnings about the cause of the flight of the Mexican domestic staff notwithstanding, the afternoon had passed uneventfully until five o'clock. Then, while Clint had been telling those of the guard force not already on duty about the precautions he wanted taken during the hours of darkness, one of the lookouts from the main gate had arrived with disturbing news. A large body of well-armed *bandidos* had put in an appearance. They had advanced cautiously, under cover that would allow them to completely surround the building. Among their other weapons were three Colt 1898 model machine guns, showing they were in deadly earnest. Although they were obsolete, the latter armament would at least counter and could possibly nullify the support offered by the defenders' more modern Brownings.

When the telephone had rung, Brickhouse had raised no objection to Torreson's offer to take the call.

Nor had Clint.

Now the small Texan could see he had made a deadly serious mistake—one likely to cost the small Texan and his *amigo* dearly!

Although Blood had the Holland & Holland .375 magnum sporting rifle across the crook of his left arm, he could not hope to be granted sufficient time to turn it into alignment before the man who had joined the New Yorker opened fire at him.

No matter how swiftly Clint could draw and use the big Colt

automatic, particularly as Torreson had cocked the hammer of
the double action manually, he knew he could not do so fast
enough to save himself from being shot.

"You heard me!" the New Yorker snarled, remembering what
he had been told was to be the fate of the two Texans and
therefore wanting to deliver them alive to Guevara. "Drop those
g—"

"You bastard, Torreson!"

Wildersleeve, who had been handing around cups of coffee,
shouted the words and lunged forward, dropping the tray. Such
was the concentrated fury and hatred expressed by his tone and
demeanor that he took everybody—especially the man to whom
he had spoken—by surprise. Upon reaching the New Yorker, he
grabbed hold of the Colt by the barrel and began to pull at it.

Snarling out a startled and alarmed profanity, Torreson tried
to wrench the weapon free. In doing so, his forefinger tightened
on the trigger. With the hammer fully cocked, the pressure required to open fire was much less than when making use of the
double-action, self-cocking mechanism. As the Colt roared and
flung its bullet into the center of the valet's chest, he was pitched
backward. The muzzle had been so close that the fiery blast of
the discharging powder singed the front of his normally spotless
white shirt.

Much of the urgency behind Torreson's actions had sprung
from a frightening realization of what exactly Wildersleeve's
intervention implied. Sure enough, as the valet was reeling
away, he discovered that Clint had not hesitated before starting
to try to capitalize upon the diversion. Raw fear of the consequences bit into the New Yorker, and he desperately began to
turn back his deflected weapon.

The attempt was to no avail.

Setting his feet apart to roughly the width of his shoulders
and slightly bending his knees, the small Texan adopted the
somewhat crouching posture that allowed him to attain the
maximum speed possible with a shoulder holster. In just six-

tenths of a second, the Colt automatic was free and in action. Its first shot was discharged an instant before the revolver could come around sufficiently far to endanger him. Five times, so rapidly the explosions merged into a continuous roar, bullets left the muzzle of the Colt. Each was sent upon a course slightly divergent from the one that preceded it. Two missed, but the remainder found their billet in Torreson's body. Driven backward by them, he disappeared into the library where he collapsed dying by the desk.

Nor did the New Yorker's sole supporter fare any better.

Startled by the unexpected turn of events, the hardcase was goaded into motion by the sight of the deadly black automatic pistol being brought into action. He should have kept the dark Texan under constant observation, but he had failed to do so. What was more, he compounded his folly by starting to turn his revolver toward Clint when Torreson's fate became obvious.

Instantly Blood sprang away from his companion. While doing so, he was bringing the rifle from his left arm and swinging the barrel to the front.

Becoming aware of his terrible error, the hardcase tried to correct it by reversing the direction of the revolver.

There was no time for Blood to raise the rifle to shoulder level and make use of its telescopic sight. Nor was there any need.

Operating the bolt with the deft speed and precision of long training, Blood aimed at waist level and by instinctive alignment. The method proved sufficient for his needs. Although the silencer caused the detonation to come as a hiss instead of a crack, there was little reduction in the velocity of the high-powered cartridge. Hit between the eyes by a bullet potent enough to stop a charging rhinoceros in its tracks, the skull of the hardcase appeared to disintegrate. For a moment his body remained erect. Then, to the accompaniment of a scream from Rita—who had been helping Wildersleeve—it crumpled as if it had been boned. It was followed down by Rita, fainting from the horror of the sight.

"All right!" Clint barked, pulling out the second automatic, which had been tucked into the right side of his waistband. "Who-all else figures on handing us over to Guevara?"

Before any reply could be made, one of the Browning machine guns in the rooms upstairs began to fire. Then the other and the rifles of the men at the gates joined in, their efforts being echoed by shots from beyond the walls.

"Hey, down there!" a voice yelled from the upper floor. "They've started throwing lead at us!"

"It doesn't look like Guevara's going to give you-all a chance to turn us over, should any of you be *loco* enough to try," Blood pointed out, holding his rifle ready for use. "Let's go and get us in some shooting back at them!"

# 16
# THEY'RE TEXAS RANGERS, RAPIDO

"What do you think of our chances, Mr. Clint?" Albert Brick-house inquired after he, the small Texan, and Comanche Blood had finished eating. Brickhouse had lowered his voice to little more than a whisper and glanced furtively at the door of the library as an indication that he had no wish for the question to be overheard by anybody outside.

"They're no better than *you're* figuring, Mr. Brickhouse," Rapido Clint replied just as quietly.

On leading the way upstairs after the killing of Victor Torreson and the other hardcase, the small Texan had demanded rather than asked what had made the men there start shooting. He was told that the Mexicans had suddenly opened fire without any provocation, so they had replied in kind. Studying the situation from various windows, seeing and being seen by Cristóbal Guevara at one—although neither had been able to take any offensive action against the other—he had failed to discover any reason why the *bandidos* had commenced hostilities. They were keeping to their places of concealment and making no attempt to move closer. Furthermore, their shooting had been brought to an end before he had completed his tour.

Going back to the ground floor with the majority of the *Hacienda Naranja*'s defenders, having left Blood behind with orders to keep an eye on things, Clint had turned the inexplicable situation to good use. Aware that the issue might arise later, he had cast doubts upon the assertion by the now-dead fugitive from New York that Guevara had offered to withdraw peacefully if he and his *amigo* were handed over. Nor had he left it at that, but had suggested that somebody try to contact the leader of the *bandidos* to learn the truth of the matter. As nobody had shown any inclination to chance making direct contact under a flag of truce, the financier had been requested to use the telephone. The discovery that the wire had been cut had seemed to support the small Texan's claim. Clint had explained its destruction by suggesting it was done to prevent any mention of the attack being made to the previous caller.

Whether Clint's comments had been accepted unreservedly or not, no attempt was made to challenge them. Nor was the question raised of why Torreson would invent such a story. Instead, the remaining hardcases had shown no hesitation before obeying the orders Clint had given regarding the part each was to play in the defense of the *hacienda*.

There had been no further attempts to contact the defenders. Nor had Clint expected there would be.

By deliberately allowing himself to be seen by Guevara, the small Texan had let it be known that Torreson had failed to compel Blood and himself to surrender. He had also ensured that precautions would be taken against any further offers being made of a similar nature.

Showing considerable perception, Blood had drawn the required conclusions from the way in which his instructions were worded. While his companion had been keeping the majority of the hardcases occupied downstairs, he had put to good use the potential for accuracy and almost noiseless discharge offered by

the telescopic sight and silencer fitted to his Holland & Holland
.375 magnum sporting rifle. After selecting a position from
which he could fire unnoticed, he had contrived to sever the
telephone wire where it passed through a conductor fastened to
a branch of a tree about a hundred yards beyond the perimeter
wall. He was also to use similar tactics to dissuade an attempt to
make vocal contact. Seeing a *bandido* starting to raise a stick to
which a white shirt was attached, he had opened fire and caused
it to be withdrawn before it attracted anybody else's attention.

Night had fallen with the situation unchanged.

When satisfied there was sufficient light from the moon to
prevent anybody approaching the walls without being detected,
Clint had allowed the defenders to leave their posts in rotation
and eat the food prepared for them by Rita Ansell. At his suggestion, the financier had waited until everybody else was finished and then joined Blood and himself in the library for their
meal. The question he had been asked when they had finished
eating was something he had expected, and it proved that
Brickhouse's thoughts on their state of affairs were running
along similar lines to Clint's own.

"You mean we can't hold out here?" the financier suggested.

"Hell, no!" the small Texan answered definitely. "Unless they
bring up one of those French Seventy-Five fellers who were with
Black Jack Pershing over there,* which are so straight shooting,
or at least a couple of old muzzle-loading cannon, none of which
I figure Guevara's got to hand, we can hold out here for longer
than he'll want to chance hanging around. Only it won't end
*there*. It's what happens *after* he hollers calf rope and quits
that'll raise the water over the willows and set the herd to swimming."

---

* "French Seventy-Five": The 75-mm 1897 model field gun developed by
France. A number were used in World War I by the American Expeditionary Force, gaining a well-deserved reputation for rugged dependability and
accuracy. *J.T.E.*

"So you don't think he'll let the matter rest, even if he gives up the attack?" Brickhouse asked, drumming his fingers nervously on the table.

"He *won't*—and neither will the jaspers who'll be one good reason he can't chance sticking it out too long."

"Who do you mean?"

"The *Rurales*."

"The *Rurales*?"

"Nobody else but!" the small Texan confirmed. "Because he knows that they'll be coming on the run as soon as word gets to them what's happening here."

*"I've* nothing to fear from *them*!" the financier asserted. However, knowing the *Guardia Rurale* to be what later generations would refer to as a paramilitary law enforcement agency with jurisdiction throughout the whole of Mexico, his tone was less than confident. "They've never bothered *me*."

"They've never been given a reason to before," Clint pointed out, duplicating the thoughts that were running through his employer's mind.

"And they *still* haven't!" Brickhouse claimed, but with a discernible lack of conviction. "It's no crime for a man to defend his life and property against an attack by thieves and murderers."

"Except when the said thieves and murderers are Mexicans!" Clint began.

"I'm a *tax-paying* Mexican citizen—" the financier started to say, but was not allowed to finish.

"Only by naturalization," the small Texan reminded the financier, although merely expressing the matter uppermost in his boss's considerations. "And, like you-all told us when we got here, there's some down to Mexico City who'd not be sorry was there a reason to rescind it. Once *that's* done, there's not one single, solitary thing to stop those folks in New York from having you extradited and brought to them."

"What do you have in mind?" Brickhouse inquired, becoming

brisk and businesslike as Blood crossed to the door to ensure the conversation was not overheard by anybody outside the library.

"That you, Comanch', the girl, and I get out of here tonight and head for someplace a whole heap safer."

"The *girl*?"

"I figured you'd want it that way. Unless I'm reading the sign about you all wrong, you've got it fixed so that not too much of your cash is tied down here in case, which was always on the cards to happen, you had to light a shuck for the deep and piney woods. Wherever you set up house again, you'll not be likely to get a gal who fights as well as she does or's as willing to do it."

"I won't at that!" Brickhouse admitted, remembering the comments the brunette made about her love of fighting. "But will she be able to come with us?"

"That gal's got sand to burn," Clint claimed. "Happen she gets told what to expect from one side or the other should she stay behind, I reckon she'll be ready to come along. Anyways, we can always leave her behind happen she can't keep up with us."

"Very well," the financier assented. "Go and see what she wants to do, please. I've got some things that I have to do— But how are we going to get out?"

"The same way you was going to tell us about when Guevara brought the *remuda* back," the small Texan replied, in the manner of one stating the obvious. "Which I'm willing to bet is through a secret passage."

"It is," Brickhouse confirmed, showing he was impressed by the latest example of the *big* young Texan's acumen. "But how did you know there was one?"

"The old-time *caballeros* who had these *haciendas* built weren't what you'd call real trusting jaspers," Clint explained. "They had their homes made like forts and, knowing even forts can be taken, made good and sure there was another way out besides the gates in the walls. I'd guess the tunnel starts in the cellar. Where does it come out?"

"In the woods on the ridge about a mile to the south." Brick-house answered without hesitation. "It's a remarkable piece of engineering, and I arranged for it to be put into working condition without any of the others, even Torreson, learning of its existence." Some of his air of smug satisfaction died away as a thought struck him and he went on in a more subdued fashion. "But there's one thing wrong with going out that way. Even if we could bring horses into the house without arousing suspicion, there's no way we could take them through the tunnel."

"I didn't reckon there would be," the small Texan declared, exuding confidence. "The greasers didn't come here on foot, so they'll have all the horses we need. You can count on good ole Comanch' there to be able to get us four of them."

"I won't promise to wide-loop that big white stallion of Guevara's," Blood said, looking around and speaking with certainty. "But I'll get some that'll be able to tote us well away from here before anybody, inside or out, knows we're gone."

"How're you making out, Miss Ansell?" Rapido Clint inquired in an amiably solicitous tone, turning in his saddle and looking at the brunette.

"I've felt better," Rita Ansell replied, trying to make her aching body more comfortable. "Like when Daisy Extall had me on the ground and was kicking me in the apples."

"You surely gave her some of that back, though," Comanche Blood remarked, throwing an admiring look at the girl.

"I know," Rita admitted, managing a smile. "But it doesn't make me feel a whole lot better to think about it at the moment."

On being informed of the intended clandestine departure from the *Hacienda Naranja,* the brunette had agreed to go along and had stated that she had done sufficient riding to avoid delaying their flight. Knowing her own clothing would not be suitable for such a journey, she had raised no objection to donning the masculine attire that Clint acquired from the rooms of the hardcases. Despite how long these preparations took, Albert Brickhouse was still not ready to leave when she had accompanied the small Texan to the ground floor.

Coming from the library, the financier proved to have changed from his Mexican garments. A black bowler was on his head and he had shown foresight in the way he was dressed. Like the hat, his black jacket, riding breeches, and boots would be more suitable for riding to hounds on a fox hunt in the eastern United States than escaping from enemies, but they and the matching open-necked dark-blue shirt and silk cravat had the advantage of being inconspicuous in the darkness. Attached to his left wrist by a thin steel chain was a bulging black briefcase secured by two combination locks. Under his arm was a brown leather tube about six inches in circumference and four feet long, fitted with a carrying handle. Questioned about them by Clint, he had said the former contained money to supply their needs until safety was reached and the latter held his collection of paintings.

Despite being narrow and smelling musty, once the entrance —which was disguised as the head of a large wine keg identical to those on either side of it—was opened and closed behind them, passing through the secret passage had posed no problems. Nor had any arisen at the exit. This was through a carefully made door merging into the rear of a small cave, the opening to which was concealed behind a clump of bushes.

Leaving the others in the cave, Blood had justified Clint's faith in his ability by returning about ninety minutes later with four horses. When the small Texan had commented upon each animal having a double-girthed Texas range saddle instead of a Mexican rig, the reply had been that they were undoubtedly property stolen from some unfortunate citizens of the Lone Star State. In which case, Blood felt he had even less cause for remorse over having to kill the two *bandidos* he had found sleeping instead of doing their duty by keeping watch on the *remuda*. After saying he realized their deaths could not be avoided, Clint had stated this meant no time must be wasted before leaving the vicinity.

While Blood was carrying out the assignment, Clint and Brickhouse discussed the immediate future of the party. The majority of the decisions, however, had been made by the small Texan. Warning that there would be pursuit by both the *bandidos* and the deserted hardcases once their departure was discovered, he had said the best way to avoid being captured was to do the unexpected. Rita had expected the financier to object on being informed that, after they had circled around Guevara's men, they would head north and cross the Rio Grande into Texas. Instead of pointing out the dangers inherent to them in returning to the United States, Brickhouse had declared this was what he had had in mind. Provided they took care along the way, they could reach a major city from which he would set about arranging for them to leave the country and establish a fresh hideout, possibly in Brazil.

Once the party had set out, it was soon obvious that any delays that occurred would not be caused by Rita. While it was evident that she was far from over the effects of her long and brutal fight, which was not helped by being on the back of a horse, she had shown herself to be a competent rider. In fact, she had won the admiration of the two young Texans by her stoical acceptance of what they realized must be considerable punishment in spite of the comparatively leisurely pace at which they were compelled to travel.

It had been Brickhouse who forced the party to restrict the pace of their flight. He was no horseman, preferring to make journeys by motor, rail, or air transport. Being so heavy, his lack of skill had thrown such a strain upon his mount that it was unable to move at the speed any of the others would have been capable of producing.

Due to the financier's incapability and the lateness of the hour at which they had set off from the *Hacienda Naranja,* the party had not reached the Rio Grande until shortly after sunrise. Nor,

considering Brickhouse's incompetence where riding was concerned, had Clint considered it safe to start the crossing before
full daylight arrived. The delay had not endangered them. Their
departure may not have been discovered, the hardcases might
not have been permitted to inform the *bandidos* of it, or the
unexpected route they had taken might have thrown off any
pursuit. Whichever was the reason, they had arrived on the
bank of Texas without opposition.

Having continued their journey, crossing the road that went
by the Premier Chicken Ranch some five miles beyond the entrance to its canyon, the party was heading in a northeasterly
direction through fairly dense wooded country when the small
Texan's question evoked a spirited response from Rita.

"We'd best rest up a spell, Rapido," Blood suggested, looking
around the clearing the party was entering and which he considered was suitable for their needs. "The hosses can stand it, even
if this tough li'l gal doesn't have to."

"This 'tough li'l gal' needs it far more than *they* do!" the
brunette asserted, but not in a complaining fashion. "In fact, I
could use all the rest I can get, preferably in a deep and soft
feather bed. But I don't suppose I'll get any."

"You *don't* suppose right," Clint confirmed, swinging from
the saddle of his stolen horse. "Not yet a-whiles, anyway. But
you-all can sit down and take it easy while Comanch' and I take
care of these fool critters."

Dismounting hurriedly and with a sigh of relief, Brickhouse
held his horse's reins in Blood's direction. They were accepted
in a way that expressed, without the need for words, the recipient's feelings for a man who would not care for his own mount.
Despite her remark, the brunette declined Clint's offer to take
her horse. Instead, she led it herself and accompanied the Texans with the other animals toward the small stream that ran
along the northeastern side of the open ground. While the financier pulled a hip flask from the inside pocket of his jacket and,

removing its top, raised it to his lips, the trio waited for the horses to cool before allowing them to drink.

"Whereabouts is the nearest town?" Rita inquired.

"Socorro's along the ways a mite," Clint replied, making a gesture with his left hand to indicate the required direction. "But we won't be going th—"

The words came to an end as half a dozen armed men wearing cowhand clothes, but each having a silver star in a circle badge pinned to the left breast of his shirt, appeared among the trees at the south side of the clearing. They were on foot and the oldest of them was accompanied by a large bluetick coonhound.

"They're Texas Rangers, Rapido!" Blood yelled, releasing the reins of Brickhouse's horse. "Beat it!"

Grabbing the low horn, as Blood was doing with his mount, Clint swung swiftly into the saddle. Blood also set his horse into motion. Splashing through the stream, the two young men rode swiftly into the woodland.

Although Brickhouse let out a yell of alarm and started to run in her direction, Rita made no attempt to duplicate the Texans' means of taking a hurried departure. Instead, she gave the financier's horse a slap on the rump, which caused it to set off after them. However, although her action clearly had been intended to prevent the financier escaping from the approaching Texas Rangers, it proved to have been unnecessary.

"Lightning!" the elderly peace officer barked as soon as Brickhouse commenced his flight. "Take him!"

Springing forward with a rapidity that suggested the reason for it having been given such a name, the big bluetick was catching up with its quarry as he was beginning to bellow a protest to the brunette's treacherous behavior. Rising in a bound, it closed its powerful jaws upon Brickhouse's right arm and its weight threw him to the ground. Showing a lack of common sense as he was in a state of panic, he struggled, and this caused the dog to hold on all the tighter.

"Call that ornery critter off, Jubal!" commanded the best-dressed of the newcomers as, paying no attention whatsoever to the departing pair of young Texans, they converged upon the trapped financier.

"Aw shucks, Maj' Tragg," the elderly peace officer answered. "Can't I let him just chomp awhiles longer, for all those good folks back East's that son of a bitch cheated out of their savings?"

"How long are you going to keep me here?" asked the girl who had called herself Rita Ansell but had admitted to another surname when it had become obvious this was known to the Texas Rangers.

"Wouldn't go so far's to say you're being 'kept' anyplace, Miss Yarborough," Sergeant Jubal Branch replied, sitting at the other side of the table in the living room of the small cabin to which the brunette had been brought. "We'n's figured, you looking like you've had one hell of a beating just recent', you'd likely sooner ride comfortable in a car to El Paso than a horse. 'Specially after how you showed you wanted to help us catch that fat jasper, Brickhouse. Which same fetches up something else, such's why'd you-all do it?"

"As you know my name, you probably know why," Rita said quietly. "He was responsible for the death of my parents."

"And you-all figured to nail his hide to the wall," Branch suggested.

"*Nobody* else seemed able to do it," the brunette answered. Because she was far from proud of her thwarted intentions where the "nailing of the financier's hide to the wall" was concerned, she went on. "When he had to leave Mexico, I came along to make sure he was arrested before he could get out of the United States again."

Which was true, as far as it went! In fact, however, the whole story went *much* farther!

When investigations instigated by Rita's father—a prominent and successful businessman—had threatened to expose

Brickhouse's machinations, Victor Torreson was hired to kill him. The attack upon Gaylord Yarborough took place as he was driving his wife to church on a Sunday afternoon, and she too had met her end in the hail of gunfire. Not that the double murder had achieved its purpose. The discoveries already made had brought about a complete exposure of the financier's numerous illegal activities, but had failed to lead to his apprehension. Realizing how close the authorities were coming, he had transferred his assets elsewhere. Having already taken the precaution of obtaining Mexican citizenship, he had fled to the *Hacienda Naranja,* which he had purchased and maintained for use in such an emergency. It had pleased his vanity to live so close to the United States border, secure in his immunity from extradition.

Realizing that Brickhouse could not be touched by the law, Rita had sworn to avenge her parents' murders personally. An intelligent girl who had always led an active life, she was fortunate in having had the financial means to acquire all she required for her scheme. Knowing of the financier's obsession with women fighting, she had decided to use this trait as a means of gaining his confidence. She had been helped by Wildersleeve's liking for her parents and hatred for his present employer. In fact, the valet had set her father on Brickhouse's trail in the first place, and she could not have achieved as much as she did without his assistance. It had been he who had told her of the plans for the special "entertainment" at the *fiesta,* while making a visit to El Paso ostensibly to purchase supplies for it unobtainable in Mexico. She had been living in the city, waiting for just such an opportunity. Learning how the combatants were to be acquired, she had put to use information gathered from two prostitutes—who had lost all their savings as a result of Brickhouse's machinations—and obtained "employment" at the Premier Chicken Ranch. Having learned of Daisy Extall's ways on the night of her arrival, she had been able to arrange that the two women were selected for the *fiesta* entertainment.

Upon reaching the *hacienda* and attaining her primary purpose, Rita had intended to inflict summary punishment upon Brickhouse. The still-unexplained disappearance of the vial of poison, which had a curare base and would have given the impression that its recipient had died in his sleep,* had prevented her from completing her mission. Thwarted, she had decided to accept his invitation to flee with him for the reason she had given Branch.

Although the rest of the Texas Rangers had escorted the financier to El Paso, the elderly sergeant had brought the brunette to what he had told her was a ranch's line shack. It was unoccupied. Despite being grateful for an opportunity to sit on something more stable than a horse, she could not resist seeking the information that had in turn started the conversation.

Before either Rita or Branch could say any more, they heard horses approaching. The hoofbeats halted, leather creaked, and footsteps came toward the door.

Glancing at the bluetick, which had been sprawling on the floor since their arrival with such an attitude of somnolence that she was barely able to recognize it as the same animal which had tackled and badly bitten Brickhouse, the brunette decided it must know whoever had arrived. It did no more than lift its

---

* "Curare," also known as *woorali,* or *urare:* A brittle, blackish, resinous extract of certain South American trees of the genus *Strychnos,* especially *S. Toxifera,* used by the native Indians as an exceptionally swift-acting arrow poison. In medical practice, it is employed as an adjunct to general anaesthesia on occasion. Curare relaxes the end plates between the nerves and muscles, preventing the heart and lungs from functioning, thereby causing death by asphyxiation. Although Alvin Dustine "Cap" Fog *claims* he does not know from where Rita "Ansell" Yarborough obtained the poison, he suggests it was probably supplied by a victim of Albert Brickhouse who was in a position to obtain it. As the lady in question eventually became Cap's wife, we find his apparent lack of information on the subject even at this late date understandable. *J.T.E.*

head a couple of inches and wag its tail briefly a few times as the door opened and two men walked in.

Which struck Rita as being very strange, for the new arrivals were Rapido Clint and Comanche Blood!

# 17
# SERGEANTS ALVIN FOG AND MARK SCRAPTON

"Hey there, Lightning, you fool old cuss!" greeted the small Texan, showing neither alarm nor surprise at finding himself in the presence of a Texas Ranger. "I know you're right pleased to see us, but quit all that rampaging and fussing before you-all scare Miss Yarborough."

"*You!*" the girl in question exclaimed, too flustered to notice she had been referred to by her real name and not the alias she had used all the time in the newcomers' presence.

"*Us!*" confirmed the dark young man Rita Yarborough knew as Comanche Blood.

"B-but you're *criminals*!" the brunette cried, then swung her bewildered gaze to where Sergeant Jubal Branch was still sitting at the table with complete absence of concern. "Are *you* one as well?"

"I can't right and truthful come out and say yes to that," the elderly peace officer replied. "Nor to the 'as well,' just the 'oppos-ical' being the case."

"Y-you!" Rita gasped, flopping back on to the chair from

which she had sprung when she saw who had entered the line
shack. "You mean that they—"

"Danged if I shouldn't've *knowed!*" Branch declared in tones
of exasperation, as the brunette's question ended without being
completed. "Young 'n's being what they be these days, I
should've figured neither of these varmints'd've had the perlite-
fulness to up and hinter-duce themselves like gentlemen.
They're Sergeants Alvin Fog and Mark Scrapton of the Texas
Rangers' Company Z."

Although Minnie Lassiter would not have heard of Company
Z, if she had been present, the reference to it would have confirmed her supposition that there was something out of the ordinary in so many exceptionally competent members of the Texas
Rangers being transferred to Major Benson Tragg's command.
They had been gathered together secretly, to form a special
force that would handle tasks beyond the capability of formal
law enforcement agencies. They were, in fact, to perform offi-
cially "unofficial" duties.

Having been requested to try and bring about the return of
Albert Brickhouse to the jurisdiction of the United States, Tragg
and his men had set about seeking the means to do so. They had
found a willing and helpful ally in the major's cousin. Although
the sheriff of El Paso could not go into Mexico after the financier, his sense of duty and interest in justice had led him to
establish a contact with one of the hardcases at the *Hacienda
Naranja.*

It had been Wildersleeve and not the contact who had drawn
Sheriff Granville Tragg's attention to Rita. Having made a habit
of keeping anybody from the *hacienda* under observation when
they visited El Paso, he had seen the valet visiting the brunette
and learned her identity through a sergeant of the New York
Police Department who had been sent to take charge of Brickhouse when, or if, a return to the United States was arranged.

Learning of the financier's troubles with Cristóbal Guevara
and the means by which he was hoping to circumvent them, the

Rangers had seen a way in which they might turn Victor Torreson's part in the arrangements to their advantage. Posing as a pair of wanted criminals, Alvin Fog and Mark Scrapton had set about the task of making the acquaintance of the fugitive from New York.*

Knowing that no recognizable weapons would be allowed upon the premises, "Clint" had carried the *yawara* stick as a means of defense if he found himself in a position from which his knowledge of bare-handed combat—including *ju jitsu* and *karate***—could not extract him. The fight with the three drunks had been a fortunate coincidence, but he had entered the Premier Chicken Ranch with the intention of creating a disturbance. There had been no other way by which the attention of the lookouts could be distracted for long enough to allow the raiding party to arrive undetected. Having been warned of how Minnie would react to his behavior, he had been ready for the attacks she made and had respected Branch's request that he avoid hurting her any more than was absolutely necessary.

The rescue had gone off without a hitch. Being handcuffed in the unconventional fashion had ensured that Torreson would

---

* On being assigned their duties, Sergeants Alvin Dustine Fog and Mark Scrapton adopted aliases that had been favored by their respective grandfathers, who were both noted characters in the Old West throughout the mid-1800s. Details of the careers of Dustine Edward Marsden "Dusty" Fog and the Ysabel Kid are supplied in various volumes of the Civil War and Floating Outfit series. An occasion when the former called himself Rapido Clint is told in *Beguinage Is Dead!* The latter made use of the sobriquet Comanche Blood during the events recorded in *Hell in the Palo Duro, Go Back to Hell, The South will Rise Again,* and Part Three, The Ysabel Kid in, "Comanche Blood," *The Hard Riders. J.T.E.*
** Alvin Dustine Fog's instructor in the use of *ju jitsu, karate,* and the *yawara* stick was a nephew of Tommy Okasi, a *samurai* who acted as valet for General Jackson Baines "Ole Devil" Hardin, C.S.A. Details of both their careers are given mainly in the Ole Devil Hardin series. More information regarding the *yawara* stick can be found in *Ole Devil and the Caplocks. J.T.E.*

have his back turned when Clint made the "attack" on Sergeant
Hans "Dutchy" Soehnen. He had failed to see that the blow was
struck with the forearm and not the *yawara* stick, the blood
being produced from an easily punctured vial of suitably colored
liquid such as was used for makeup in the theater. The Colt
Government model automatic pistols carried by Soehnen belonged to Clint, and the one with which he was "shot" had been
loaded with bullets made of wax.* Being partially melted by the
heat of the ignited powder and passage through the barrel, these
had made the holes in his vest. They were prevented from pene-
trating his body by striking a sheet of metal hidden inside his
shirt. Torreson had been taken away by the two young Texans
before he had an opportunity to examine the "body" or notice
there was no blood from the wounds.

Later, Branch had realized that Minnie was curious about the
presence of so many prominent and senior Texas Rangers in the
raiding party. With an eye on the future of Company Z, which
depended on its existence being prevented from becoming public
knowledge, he had supplied the hint to Major Tragg that had
kept Soehnen "alive," albeit supposedly wounded.

From the moment of their arrival at the *Hacienda Naranja,*
Clint and Blood had been on the alert for ways in which they
could ingratiate themselves with Brickhouse and cause dissen-
sion among the hardcases. The "theft" of the *remuda* had been
carried out by Sergeants Carlos Franco and Alexandre
"Frenchie" Giradot, the latter disguised as a Mexican and the
former doing all the talking. Having done so, they had driven
the horses until they had been seen and "chased off" by some of
Guevara's men. The leader of the *bandidos* had then returned
the animals to their owners.

It had been the Texans' intention to provoke Guevara into

---

* Another occasion when Alvin Dustine Fog posed as Rapido Clint and
made use of wax bullets is recorded in *"Cap" Fog, Texas Ranger, Meet Mr.
J.G. Reeder. J.T.E.*

attacking the *hacienda*. Nor, being aware of the ruthless and vicious nature of the men with whom they were dealing, had they felt any qualms over the treatment accorded to Che Orlando and *el Toro*. Although Guevara had hoped to avert a gun battle by making a show of strength and demanding the surrender of Clint and Blood as the price of his departure, this possibility had been taken into account. Having remained in the vicinity and kept out of sight, Franco and Giradot had fired shots in the direction of both parties on seeing hostilities were not being commenced.

The Texans' belief that the *hacienda* had a secret exit was confirmed by Brickhouse when the horses were "stolen," although Guevara's arrival to return them had prevented him from mentioning it in the presence of the hardcases. If this had not happened, however, Clint had intended to stop him making the disclosure. Satisfied there was a way of leaving, it had only remained for them to persuade the financier to accompany them after the attack took place. This had not been difficult. Realizing that his stay in Mexico was likely to be terminated by the authorities—using the fighting as an excuse—or made unhealthy by Guevara, he had been only too willing to accept Clint's suggestion.

Being aware that Rita was not what she pretended to be, the small Texan had contrived to include her in the party. This had provided Franco and Giradot with something of an inconvenience, as they had only brought three spare horses with them. On hearing of the unanticipated development when Blood had met them at a prearranged rendezvous, their solution was to hand over Giradot's mount and ride double on the horse belonging to Franco.

All that had remained for the two young Texans to do was deliver Brickhouse to the clearing in Texas where their comrades-in-arms were waiting to collect him and make good their own "escape" so he would not suspect how he had been tricked. This had been accomplished satisfactorily, leaving them free to join Branch at the line shack and find out if there were any fresh instructions for them.

"Would this be what I think it is, Miss Yarborough?" Clint inquired, bringing from his jacket's inside pocket the small vial of poison he had discovered at the time he had been trying to learn what she meant to do with regard to the financier.

"So it was *you* who took it!" Rita gasped, her expression confirming the small Texan's suspicions with regards to the vial's contents.

"I thought it would be for the best," Clint declared. "New York wanted him alive and, unless I'm mistaken, there'll be everything in the briefcase he had chained to him that they'll need to lay their hands on his money.*

"Do you-all reckon you could have gone through with it?" Blood wanted to know, having reached the same conclusion as his *amigo* while watching the brunette's reactions.

"I'm not sorry the need didn't arise," Rita admitted. "But, after what he caused to happen to my parents, I feel sure I *could* have. The way things stood, there was nothing could be done to him legally."

"That's right frequent' the case, this-all being a democracy we live in," Branch asserted. "Which's why Company Z's been formed. Any time the legal law can't throw and hawg-tie some slicker, we're to go in and get the son of a bi—*gun* regardless."**

---

* While Cap Fog's assumption proved correct, there is nothing in the records of the case we have seen to suggest what happened to Albert Brickhouse's collection of paintings. *J.T.E.*

** Because of the unconventional nature of their duties, the State Legislature of Texas still considers it is politic to disclaim all knowledge of Company Z's formation and operations. A further case that required the kind of handling to which Sergeant Jubal Branch referred is recorded in the next volume of the Alvin Dustine "Cap" Fog series: *The Justice of Company Z.* *J.T.E.*